Save the horses, Sara!

Anna Sellberg

Save the horses, Sara!

Copyright © Anna Sellberg 2004
Original title: Rädda hästarna, Sara!
Cover layout: Stabenfeldt AS
Translated by Tore Fauske

Published by PonyClub, Stabenfeldt 2004
Edited by Karen Pasacreta
Printing: GGP Media, Poessneck
ISBN: 82-591-1150-0

Chapter 1

It rained. Cats and dogs. It splashed and gushed down from the dark, cloudy sky. The car's windshield wipers worked at full speed, back and forth, back and forth – even so, they didn't manage to clear away the wall of water pouring down.

"Oh man!" mumbled Dad and eased the throttle up even more. "Can you believe this rain? I can't see a darn thing."

I nodded silently. Already in a bad mood, the awful rain didn't help. I was soaked to the skin, my blonde, shoulder-length hair hanging in ugly wet strands. I shuddered and sighed.

Dad and I were on our way home from a cross-country ride – a club competition arranged by the riding club about eight miles from home.

It had been a long day, with a very early start. My pony, Fandango, had been in great form when we left that morning! I had plaited his short, dark mane; the gray coat shined brightly, and his eyes sparkled as he bounced out from the stable as he spotted the horsebox. Like me he loved competitions, and we had looked forward to this cross-country ride for several weeks.

It was overcast when we loaded Fandango into the horsebox and moved slowly away from the yard. But that didn't matter, I thought – on the contrary – it might be an advantage since we were to compete.

But the drizzle did not cease at all, as the weather report had promised the previous day. Instead, the rain had become heavier and heavier, and towards lunchtime, when it was our turn to start, it was more like a torrent. And when we galloped towards the first obstacle, an attractive little birch oxer right on the edge of the forest, the heavens opened!

When Fandango and I crossed the finishing line after having jumped the 12 obstacles, both of us were soaking wet, sweaty, and exhausted!

Dad ran toward us, nearly as wet and fed-up as I was after having just completed the course – galloping flat out.

"Hurry!" he shouted. "I'll wait near the horsebox!"

I steered Fandango towards the parking area, a long way away, while Dad took a shortcut through the woods and over two barbed wire fences. When we arrived it didn't take a minute to get Fandango into the horsebox; he seemed pleased to get away from the rain.

I took the saddle, bridle, and all the bits and pieces, and chucked them in a heap into the back of the car, while Dad gave my pony some much deserved hay and tepid water. Soon, Fandango ate happily away, without a care in the world.

I really wanted to start for home right away, but Dad felt we ought to have a quick snack first – and see who had won. He also said that we were among the fastest, so I began to hope for a rosette. I thought we deserved it, we really did, especially bearing in mind the awful weather.

We hurried over to the cafeteria – only to discover that

we didn't have any money for a snack! I had used my last to pay the entry fee – and Dad, of course, had left his wallet at home. Typical!

As it happened, we had started as one of the last competitors, so it took only about 20 minutes before it was clear we were second. The award ceremony was short and sweet; everyone was as soaked to the skin and as fed up as we were, and only wanted to get home with their tired horses.

"Congrats on a splendid victory!" said the woman handing out the prizes, an elderly, short-haired lady and member of the competition committee, giving the prize to the rider who had won that day – none other than Fredrik Carlson.

Those nearest applauded, but I just stared straight ahead. I could feel how Fredrik looked disapprovingly at me, and I would bet anything that he looked just as overconfident as he always did! Imagine that he and Buzy Bee had beaten Fandango and me – for once! "He'll be remembering that one for a long time, the jerk," I thought, feeling less than happy.

Then it was my turn to receive a blue rosette, and the ceremony was over shortly afterwards. And here I was in the car, feeling rotten. Not so much because we had taken second place, because that was more than I had expected, but because Fredrik Carlson, of all people, had won!

So just who is this Fredrik Carlson, you may ask? He's my age, and the two of us have always detested each other.

Fredrik is handsome – or at least he thinks so! He has blue eyes and blond, curly hair, and thinks he's God's gift to all girls. And he's keen on horses and competitions – just like me.

We have been in the same class at school for many years,

7

and also meet at the same competitions on weekends, without becoming friends or getting to know each other any better. One reason is that Fredrik is a member of the "in-crowd," which I am not. But I nearly always win whenever we compete against each other – but I'm sure he'd rather die than ever admit that.

Fredrik's ponies have always been looked after by the riding school, so he doesn't have to lift a finger himself. There always seems to be enough starry-eyed, love-lorn stable girls only too eager to groom his competition ponies, or walk them around the muddy field, while Fredrik enjoys a snack in the cafeteria, all the while bragging to his friends. And should one girl finally get fed up, there are at least seventeen other girls lining up to offer their assistance!

Ah, well, I suppose I could have lived with all this, somehow. You can't love everyone in this world, and although Fredrik sent some rather sarcastic comments now and then in my direction, at school or during competitions, I didn't take them to heart, but returned the compliments. So in general we tried to avoid each other.

But there is one thing about Fredrik I really cannot stand and intensely detest: he is not kind to his ponies. He may look angelic, but he is a tough and uncompromising rider, often using spurs, whip, and a sharp bit. Not only that, he never, ever pats his pony or says, "Well done!" after a good round. Never! He just rides out of the arena and more or less flings the reins to a stable girl or to his mom instead of taking care of the pony himself. I don't call that a good horseman!

So in spite of the fact that Fandango had been very good and jumped like a champion, I was really upset that we didn't beat Fredrik.

I sat in silent gloom, staring into the pouring rain until we turned into our courtyard.

Our other two horses, well, one pony and one horse to be exact, were standing in the rain next to the stable, which is really a converted hen house. Camigo, my little white roan pony, lifted his head, neighing excitedly, when he spotted us. And Dad's old competition horse, Maverick, a bay, also displayed some interest when we stopped in the yard. They say old circus horses can still smell the sawdust, so perhaps he remembered former days on the competition course with Dad – or perhaps he simply wanted to get into his box, away from the incessant rain, and have some hay. I guessed the latter, while Dad undoubtedly was convinced about the former.

We hurried to get Fandango out, loading him straight into his box. Dad ran out in the rain, leading the other two in, while I removed the transport protection and cover from Fandango. He rubbed his head so heavily against me that he nearly pushed me back against the wall. At that moment, Dad came into the stables again, saw it, and sighed.

"How many times have I told you not to do it like that? One day he'll give you a real hard blow!"

"Oh please," I said and walked out of the box. "It's OK!"

Dad is a real worrier, he really is! Worrying about everything and nothing, all the time. And not only does he love giving the whole world good advice – he even expects the whole world to follow it! Wow!

Just at that moment Mom came into the stable.

"Ah – there you are," she said gaily. "Did everything go well?"

"Yes," I said, "we came in second. Has Mike phoned?"

"He has. He is on his way over. He tried to ring you, but got no answer."

No answer? Of course – I had completely forgotten to turn my cell phone on! I always have it on, but there it was in my pocket, dead as the doornail, and it had been like that all day. I switched it on and found a text message from Mike. It was short and simple *"Good luck!"* but more than enough to make my heart beat faster. Isn't he sweet!

"I'll go in and make you some lunch," said Mom, and the word "lunch" made me suddenly realize how hungry I was. I had not had anything to eat since breakfast, and that had been merely a glass of juice and a dry cinnamon roll, which I had found in a bag in the freezer. I put it in the microwave, which made it warm – and bone dry.

Having given all the three horses some hay, I dashed across to the house with an old plastic bag over my head as protection against the never-ending amounts of rain cascading down from above.

We were sitting in the kitchen, drinking juice, when Mike arrived on a rattling old lady's bike. In order to keep fairly dry, he had put on an enormous oilskin coat and threw on an equally enormous, and bright red, hat on top. He looked like a madman, and, as he came into the hall, our Labrador Swift, jumped up and ran towards him, furiously snarling and barking. The hairs along Swift's back pointed straight up, until he suddenly realized that the apparition was not so much an apparition but a friend – and wagged his tail instead.

I went to greet him, and as soon as Mike had managed to remove the dripping oilskin, he gave me a hug. I closed my eyes and buried my nose in Mike's sweater – it smelled beautifully of stable and horses – and some paint.

"You'd better make some more coffee," muttered Dad to Mom in the kitchen.

He didn't really like the fact that I was still seeing Mike, who worked for our neighbors, Hans and Maggie.

Or so he said! But what on earth had Mike and I to do with Dad and Hans having been at odds for years? Nothing! And all because of a trivial matter, which, over the years, had taken on what seemed like major proportions; the felling of a few trees on a wooded slope. Dad said the trees were his; Hans said they belonged to him. In the end, they had to ask someone from the local authorities to come along and measure and establish the exact borderline between the two farms. It turned out that each farm owned approximately the same number of trees – and the fee for establishing all this came to more or less the price Dad and Hans would have gotten for the trees they wanted to cut down! And what's more, the trees were still there, every one of them, since neither Dad nor Hans had gotten around to felling any of them yet.

As soon as we had sat down by the table, Dad started asking Mike about Hans and Maggie's new stables. The old one had gone up in flames the month before, and they had started building a new one. The foundations were already in place, and you could see where the walls were to be erected.

Dad pretended that he wasn't really interested – he simply asked to be polite – and yet Hans's new stables was the only thing he talked about whenever Mike was around.

"So what's happening?" he asked Mike, trying not to sound too curious. "Do you think Hans will have more boxes than before? And will the drainage arrangements from the stable be some sort of environment-friendly system, or what?"

"Maybe," said Mike. "I don't know, really. I just build what Hans tells me to build."

He brushed through his blonde hair with one hand and gave me a quick, sideways look. It was clear he did not know what to say to Dad's rather nosey questions. I sighed quietly – Dad could be a real embarrassment at times!

"Well, of course, I'm not the slightest interested!" said Dad, taking another cinnamon roll. "Why should I be? But –"

"When are we building our new stables, then?" I interrupted him. "You have promised for many years to convert the old cowsheds, and also promised that we should get a proper tack room, with heating and space for hanging soft covers and all sorts of things!"

"That's right," sighed Mom. "It would be very nice if you could hang all those horse things in a stable instead of in the cellar."

"Well, um," said Dad, "I don't know. Although – perhaps we could do it now, before school starts again?"

I looked skeptical. Did he mean it? He had been talking for ages about building new stables without anything having happened. In spite of the fact that it was more than a year since my parents sold the last calves, the cowshed was just standing there, empty and unused, but with more than ample space to make superb stables! And not only that, at a right angle to the old cowshed was an old stable-part in bricks, which could easily be converted to an equally superb tack room.

"Are you joking?" I said suspiciously.

Dad cleared his throat and shook his head.

"No, not at all. I have really been thinking about this for some time. You'll get a bigger horse once we find a good one, and – well, yes, I know I promised."

"Let's go out and have a look now!" I said enthusiastically.

"OK," agreed Dad right away, and a few minutes later he, Mike, and I hurried as fast as we could across the yard and over to the cowshed in the downpour.

Dad opened the door and we stumbled in over the threshold. The pens and the feeding trays for the calves were still there. The cowshed had been cleaned out a long time ago, but there was still a definite smell of cattle. And a thick layer of dust had settled on everything. And not only dust, Mom and Dad had used the shed as a storage, or "dumping" shed, for anything under the sun; chairs, old paint cans, dried up and hardened paint brushes, my little sister Sophia's old bike, a torn mattress, Mom's fertilizer for the roses, a rickety armchair with a gaping hole, the frame of an old deck chair with pieces of material still clinging to the ends, a couple of rolled-up rugs, car parts, old tiles – you name it – What wasn't in there is hardly worth mentioning.

"This can be made to be really nice!" said Mike after having stepped carefully around and over various things. "It's just to clear it all out, build boxes – and paint it all."

"Just to clear it all," I echoed, having no difficulties in seeing the amount of work – dirty work – required. But Dad seemed to have made up his mind.

"You're quite right!" he said to Mike, straightening his back. "It will be first class stables, this will. Every bit as good as Hans's!"

It suddenly dawned on me – of course! It was the same old story: what Hans had, Dad also wanted. And if Hans's thoroughbreds were to have brand new and first-class stables, our three horses would most certainly have the same. It was as simple as that! I giggled a bit, and Mike put his arm round my shoulders.

"What's so funny?" he asked quietly while Dad walked

13

over to the far end of the shed to look at some wooen boards lying on the floor.

"I'll tell you later," I said quickly.

Mike gave me a quick hug, and I thought that next time I saw Hans, I really ought to thank him for helping me.

Chapter 2

Say what you want about Dad, but once he's made up his mind, he's made up his mind! Two days later, a large, green container appeared in the yard, and the same morning we began the task of clearing out the cowshed.

My little sister Sophia didn't help, of course. It's been a long time since she lost her interest in horses, and to get dirty clearing out an old cowshed to be made into stables was the very last thing she had in mind.

Only a few years ago, Sophia and I had always had great fun together, but over the last year we had both changed and became quite different. Sophia is two years younger than me – she's 14. She is slim, with long legs and looks any famous model would envy.

She used to ride just as much as I did, and the intention was that she would inherit my old competition pony Camigo. But lately the intervals between each ride got longer and longer.

Now she was spending most of the time with her best friend, Alexandra. I didn't always know exactly what they were up to – but I had a slight feeling that Mom and Dad wouldn't jump for joy if they got wind of the little snippets of information Sophia had hinted to me on a few occasions.

I preferred to be with the horses, walking about in my old, worn jeans and a sweater. Of course I dressed properly and put on some make-up now and then, for example whenever Mike and I went to the movies, but I wouldn't dream of wasting time on putting on make-up every day! But Sophia has a make-up box full of lipstick, mascara, blush, and whatnots. And at least *one* tube each of the many skin creams ever invented!

Sophia and Alexandra went in to town quite often, visiting shops – a total waste of time if you ask me! I buy what I need or want – and go straight home afterwards. Unless I go to the library to borrow some good books first. I love reading – preferably thick novels, which takes days to read.

So I suppose it's not all that strange that Sophia calls me a boring so-and-so whenever we argue. So what! I enjoy what I am doing, and if my little sister wants to spend all her money on anything but horses, that's up to her!

I had just chucked an old, broken chair into the garbage bin when Sophia came by on her bike, no doubt on her way to meet Alexandra, who lived on a new estate not far away.

"Mike called a minute ago," she said and stopped. She straightened her long, blonde hair and tried to pull the short, tight top down over her tummy. Sophia's way of dressing is a mixture of the latest fashion and what she regards as tough – a combination which doesn't always equal smart! Now she had on a white top, a skirt reaching well below her knees – and sneakers with enormous soles.

"You'd better take a sweater," said Mom, appearing from the stables with another broken chair. "It will get cooler later."

"Tschh – I'm not cold!" Sophia made a face.

"Perhaps not, not now – but you will be later," said Mom patiently. "Go and get a sweater."

"Oh, stop it! I –" snapped Sophia, and if I hadn't interrupted her she would undoubtedly have churned out the old theme – that she was big enough and old enough to make up her own mind. I couldn't bear the thought of it!

"What did Mike say?" I asked her.

Sophia sighed. "He's on his way over. I think he mentioned something about giving a helping hand throwing things away. Not that I can understand why, but people out here in the sticks have the strangest hobbies, so why not?"

"Wish you had!" I said, wiping the perspiration off my forehead with a dirty hand. Sophia had an irritated grin, jumped on her bike and disappeared with a "Ciao!" Without her sweater.

Mom sighed.

"Sophia has changed a great deal this summer," she said, throwing the chair she had been holding into the container. "She was such a nice and sweet little girl."

"She's still nice," I said, defending my little sister, "it's only that she hides it much more."

Mom shook her head.

"I hope she pulls herself together when school starts again. She really ought to get higher marks this term."

School! I'd rather not think about it. Not now, during the holidays. Just the thought of the school bus, morning and afternoon, long, boring lessons and a lot of homework.

At that moment Mike arrived in his little white car, which had evidently been willing to start that day. He gave me a hug.

"How are things?" he asked.

"Couldn't be better!" said Dad as he discarded the last bits of an old table into the container.

"Good," said Mike and followed me into the cowshed.

Most of the rubbish had gone, but it was still dusty and dirty everywhere.

Mike had already seen the newer part of the building, but he had never been into the old stable part of bricks, so I thought I might as well show that to him.

We went outside again, and I removed the rusty crossbar from the old, black door. The door was stuck – I had to pull with all my might before it gave way, slowly, moaning and creaking loudly.

The air inside seemed to have been there for at least a hundred years; it was thick with a musty smell of damp and dust.

"This is where the horse and a cow or two were kept," I explained to Mike as we looked around. "Then my great grandfather hit better times, and he built the new cowshed next to the stable."

"I see," said Mike with interest, peering into the darkness. "Can't you switch the light on so we can see what it looks like?"

"There's no electricity here," I said. "I'll get a flashlight."

"Don't bother – open the door wide, then we might be able to make out what's here."

It wasn't easy. Not only because of all the bits and pieces, neatly stacked and clearly forgotten, but just as much because of the layers of dust and cobwebs covering everything. The deep windowsill was a graveyard for hundreds of flies, also covered in dust and cobwebs. Suddenly I heard a rustling noise in a corner full of pieces of wood and rubbish. "Ugh! A rat!" I thought to myself.

"It will take ages to clear this away," said Mike and frowned.

18

I had to agree. It seemed close to an impossible task to turn this into a neat, clean, and useful tack room.

Just then Dad arrived, and the first thing he did was to hit his head on the low doorframe. He muttered something, which I am sure he did not intend for us to hear, and switched on a flashlight he had been wise enough to bring along.

"My God!" he exclaimed and gasped. "Some of this stuff must be from my grandfather's time. Look at that pile of old harnesses in the corner!"

The yellowish light from the torch rested on a pile of moldy leather, old bits, reins, and ropes.

I shuddered. "What a lot of old garbage!" I said.

"The question is: Wouldn't it be better to leave all this alone?" asked Mom who had come in without any of us noticing. "What about building a tack room inside the cow-shed instead, where we have both water and electricity?"

"No," said Dad very firmly. "I have decided to clear away everything in here as well. Once that's done, I'll make a door –" he gestured towards the wall – "so that we can walk straight in here from the stable and collect whatever we need."

I nodded. I thought it was good idea.

Before anyone could say anything, we heard a car turn into the yard outside and, through the dirty window, I saw it was a large, red car. It stopped next to the container, and two people got out. To my surprise I saw it was Fredrik Carlson and his mom, whose name I seemed to remember was Beatrice. They looked around, and Beatrice called out loudly: "Hello – anyone home?"

"We're in here!" shouted Dad, and trying to get out in a hurry he hit his head on the door frame again, sending a shower of dust and cobwebs like snow over his head and shoulders, making him cough and splutter. We followed, but a bit more orderly. Fredrik and his mom stared at us, and no wonder; we were all dusty, dirty, and sweaty, and Dad rubbed his forehead where yet another swelling had appeared. Mike was holding an old, dirty snaffle he had taken off a nail in the wall. We were undoubtedly quite a sight!

"We were just passing, so we thought we would call in and say hello," said Beatrice. Fredrik gave me a look, which made it more than clear that it certainly wasn't his idea!

"Well, why not?" said Dad, gently feeling the bump with his hand.

"The thing is – we are moving to this neighborhood," continued Beatrice, taking a step sideways as Swift rushed towards her, greeting her with a wagging tail.

"We won't exactly be the nearest neighbors, but, well, as I said, I thought we ought to call in and –" She stopped, trying to protect herself against Swift's somewhat close attention.

"What?!" I gasped, "You are moving over here? When? Where?" I am sure I sounded horrified, but so what?

"We bought a farm on the other side of the forest. It's called Hedeby," said Beatrice.

"Ah – so you're the ones moving in there," said Dad, brushing some dust off his jumper. "Yes, I heard that the Oscarsons had sold the farm."

"Welcome to the area," said Mom, sounding very friendly. "Will you keep horses?"

"Of course! My husband will be running a business, and we'll keep Fredrik's competition ponies at home," said Beatrice. "That is," she added, "at the moment he only has a pony, but it is time to get a big and proper horse – or horses."

Everyone was silent, and I glanced at Fredrik. He was leaning against the car, arms tightly across his chest, staring surly straight ahead.

His mom hesitated for a moment, looking for words. I guessed there was a specific reason why they had called in – not just to say "Hello," as she first said – and I was curious to know what it was. Fredrik's mom and my parents had hardly spoken this many words with each other since Fredrik and I were in the same class and they had been elected as "parent representatives" in the same year. So I thought it was strange that she should have this sudden urge to be so nice and friendly.

"We have a little problem we need some help with," said Beatrice, nodding towards Fredrik. "The riding school is still closed for summer holidays, as you may know, so we have nowhere to stable Buzy Bee, because he can't stay where he is at the moment, and our stable isn't quite ready yet." She clearly felt a bit uneasy.

"So?" said Dad, obviously totally unaware of what she was hinting at. I knew what was coming, and I pulled a face at him, taking care so Fredrik and Beatrice could not see it, as a signal to be wary. But did he understand me? HA!

"So we wondered if Fredrik might possibly be able to, that is, if he could stable Buzy Bee here for about a week?" said Beatrice, and I realized this did not come easy for her.

"Here?" said Dad, surprised, scratching his head. "Well, yes – I suppose – I can't see why not –"

I glared angrily at Dad and formed the word "NO!" silently with my mouth, but he still had no idea of what was going on!

But Mom noticed.

"What's the matter, Sara? Are you all right?" she asked, looking at me.

"What? Yes – yes. Of course I am all right! Why do you ask? I'll just continue clearing out the cowshed."

I nodded to Fredrik, who did not look all that happy either, and went back into the cowshed. Mike followed me, and when we were well out of sight he put his arms around me and gave me a hug.

"Is that the guy you can't stand?" he asked, and I nodded.

"But it's only for a few days," said Mike, stroking my hair.

I nodded again, tore myself away and started to collect a whole lot of roof tiles dumped in a heap at the far wall. Mike helped me, fully aware I was not in a buoyant mood, so he didn't say a word, only emptied the bucket into the container as I filled it.

At last, Fredrik and his mom left, and I made a face after the car as it disappeared. Dad looked quite pleased with himself.

"But what on earth is the matter with you?" he asked, surprised, when he saw me.

"You know I *hate* Fredrik Carlson!" I said, angrily and upset. "And you say he can stable his horse here – with us!"

"But Sara – it is only for a few days – no more than a week!"

"A few days or a week – it's far too long," I snapped. "You could at least have *asked* first!"

Dad looked embarrassed.

"Well, yes, perhaps I could –"

"I can't quite understand either why you said yes so readily," said Mom, who just then appeared with secateurs in one hand and a small spade in the other. "I have never liked Beatrice Carlson. It will be difficult to find a snootier person."

"I only wanted to be obliging," said Dad and looked sheepish. "It's only for a few days, and I thought it was no hardship saying yes. After all – they will be our new neighbors."

"There is no way their pony will be in with ours!" I said firmly. "He will have to be in the winter paddock."

"Oh, dear," said Dad, "I said their pony could be with Camigo since he doesn't like being on his own."

"Never!" I said. "Never! Never!" I glared at Dad. "It was you who said yes to this idiotic idea, so you can sacrifice your own horse. If this pony needs company, it will have to be Maverick!"

"But –" began Dad slowly, but I heard he had already given in.

Mike started to laugh loudly, and I looked angrily at him.

"I can hear who decides here," he said with a grin and gave me a friendly push. "Come on, let's get rid of the last tiles – then I have to leave to go over to Hans' stables."

I mumbled something, but then I couldn't help laughing. Mike and Dad were right, of course – it was only for a few days. And I would just have to try and survive those few days.

Chapter 3

The next morning, Sophia came into my room and woke me - at 9 a.m.! I knew she had come home terribly late the night before, so it surprised me that she was up and about already, looking fit and sharp.

"Dad said that Fredrik Carlson wants to have his pony here!" she beamed loudly and plunked herself down at the end of my bed. "And that we'll be neighbors."

"Neighbors?" I mumbled, trying to wake up. "Hardly neighbors – their farm is at least three miles from here. Get out! I want to sleep!"

"Don't be so rotten," said Sophia. "Fredrik is soooo nice, and Buzy Bee is gorgeous!"

"It's marvelous, isn't it?" I growled, pulling the bedcover over my head. "If you ask him on bended knees, I'm sure Fredrik will let you polish his riding boots with your toothbrush, *and* take care of his dirty pony after a ride," I said sarcastically from under the cover.

"I say, dear sister – are we in a bad mood today?"

"GET OUT OF MY ROOM!" I shouted and sat up and threw a pillow at Sophia. "JUST GET OUT! And don't come back this century!"

Sophia giggled slightly and rolled her eyes as she got up, left the room and closed the door carefully behind her. I was wide awake, of course, being a bit angry and irritated, so there was no question of going back to sleep. I gave up after a while and went downstairs into the kitchen, made a cup of hot chocolate and a sandwich, and sat down by the kitchen table to read the paper.

The door opened and Sophia came in.

"I'm thinking of taking a ride," she said. "Want to come along?"

"You? You riding?" I couldn't hide my surprise. "Why? I thought you had sworn off horses!"

"Don't be silly! I thought I'll ride over and take a look at the farm Fredrik's parents have bought, see?" Sophia took a sugar cube from the bowl.

"Are you coming or not?" she asked, crushing the cube between her teeth. "I'll bet anything you're just as curious as I am!"

I didn't reply - she had guessed correctly; I *was* curious. And shortly afterwards we were on our way, on Camigo and Fandango.

We were quite different in appearance, my little sister and I. I was wearing jodhpurs, a T-shirt, and riding shoes, and Fandango looked neat and tidy. But my dear sister, who rarely sat on horse these days, was wearing a pink tight top, jeans with a flowery pattern, and boots. Camigo had been partly groomed, and the saddle was on, but his tail was full of dry mud, and he had a large grassy mark on his belly.

"Dad will go crazy if he sees you riding about like that," I said, but Sophia only laughed.

"He's hopelessly old-fashioned, don't you think, Sis?" she said and broke a twig off a shrub as she passed it. She waved it back and forth, keeping the flies off Camigo. I did the same, and I am sure Fandango appreciated it.

We followed a graveled road to start with, but soon left that for a track into the forest. It was a beautiful August morning, and I think the horses enjoyed it as much as we did. They really seemed pleased to be out together again – it had been some time since last rode together.

Sophia hadn't been riding for several weeks, and whenever Mike and I went out riding, he normally rode Maverick. True, I did ride my old and faithful pony now and then, but the gaps were getting bigger and bigger. I have really grown too big for him, so Camigo spent most of his days just wandering around in the enclosure, eating and relaxing. It was a pity, because he was a very good competition pony; he should really be with a smaller rider who would ride him every day.

"Come – let's trot a bit," I suggested and hauled the reins in a bit. Fandango reacted immediately, but I made sure he didn't run faster than Camigo could keep up. Camigo was not so fit and in the same competitive shape, which I had to consider.

Sophia followed behind, but after only a couple of hundred feet she shouted to me to slow down.

"What's the matter?" I asked and turned round.

"Camigo is tired," said Sophia, nearly out of breath. She was very red in the face. "And it's terribly hot!"

"Pull the other one!" I said to my little sister when I saw how keen Camigo was to carry on, tossing his head from side to side, stepping sideways on the track. "It's not Camigo – you're the one who's all puffed out!"

"Shut up!" said Sophia, loosening the reins, and stopping next to Fandango and me.

It didn't take all that long to ride from home to the farm

Fredrik's parents had bought. Both Sophia and I knew the forest like the back of our hand, and the track we were following led us virtually straight to the farm.

Hedeby was quite isolated, and while riding along I wondered how Fredrik would enjoy living all the way out here. Although his dad already owned a large farm – breeding cattle – some miles from the town, the family had always lived in a rather splendid house in the center of the town.

We arrived at the gravel path leading to the farm, and from there it was only a matter of minutes before we reached the farm. There wasn't much to be curious about – nothing exciting at all. Fredrik's family had renovated the large farmhouse; it looked newly painted with bright red walls and snow-white window frames. The old cowshed had been demolished and replaced by new stables with room for three or perhaps four horses. A big pile of earth indicated that Fredrik would have a riding track, and poles showed where the enclosures were to be. But the whole place gave an air of having been abandoned – perhaps because we didn't see a single soul.

"Not bad!" said Sophia admiringly. I sighed.

"Of course it isn't bad, with all the money they have! And we aren't even talking about their house in town."

"Yes, I know," said Sophia. "But even so."

We followed the gravel path for a while. The pine forest stood dense and dark on either side, and I was just going to suggest that we should turn around and ride home when I spotted something that made me look again. A short distance in front of us, someone had made a brand new graveled road leading straight into the forest!

"Look, how strange!" I said and pointed. "Who would even think of building a new road here, in the middle of nowhere?"

"So what? It has nothing to do with us, does it?" Sophia wanted to ride home.

"Come on – I want to see where it leads to!" I said, turning Fandango onto the new road.

"It probably leads to a clearing or something. Where else?" said Sophia and sounded impatient. "Let's take off. I'm supposed to meet Alexandra and the others soon. We're going for a swim, and I don't want to be late."

"It won't take a minute to see where the road goes," I said, trying to persuade her. "Look, it's perfect for cantering!"

"As if I care!" muttered Sophia but, reluctant or not, we cantered side by side along the new road.

It wasn't very long before we came to a red and yellow barrier across the road, with a big sign saying: "No unauthorized access." We could see a large graveled area on the other side, and a large building made from grayish-green corrugated panels. A man on a large, yellow tractor was busy excavating next to the building, and three other men were erecting a fence of solid wood.

Suddenly one of the men spotted us. He was tall and well built, with gray hair and bushy eyebrows, dressed in jeans, a checkered shirt and a yellow cap with "New York" logo on it.

As he got closer I recognized him. It was Fredrik Carlson's dad, and if I remembered correctly his name was Frank.

"Hello, girls, what can I do for you?" he asked and smiled.

"Eh – well – nothing," I said. We just wondered where this new road would lead us."

Fredrik's dad stroked Camigo's muzzle and nodded towards the building. "It is going to house some machines," he said, then hesitated a bit and looked at me.

"Don't I know you?" he asked, raising his eyebrows a bit.

"I am in the same grade as Fredrik at school," I replied.

He nodded. "Of course, of course – I remember. Well, I have to get going. Bye!"

He gave us a nod, turned and walked back to the others. Sophia turned Camigo round.

"How terribly exciting!" she said and made a face. "A building for some machinery! I do hope the others will be waiting for me. It's your fault!" She sent an angry look in my direction.

"Stop it, will you?" I said. "You didn't have to come along – you could have stayed home." Then I suddenly remembered. "It was your idea in the first place that we should ride over here!"

Sophia didn't answer, and we rode side by side in total silence, glaring at each other.

We had nearly reached the other graveled road when Fandango stopped and lifted his head. We could hear engine noises – and suddenly two large, green and brown trucks came thundering towards us at great speed!

The road was narrow and, instinctively, I pulled Fandango to one side. He didn't understand at first exactly what I wanted him to do, but I shouted at him and dug my heels into his sides, and he jumped off the road and into the shallow ditch. Camigo and Sophia followed, the two trucks missing us by inches as they shot noisily past, disappearing in a cloud of sand and dust.

"Idiots!" shouted Sophia angrily, waving her fist after them. "Crazy idiots! You could have killed us!"

"Don't waste your breath," I said, trying to calm down Fandango. "They can't hear you!"

"I've never seen anything like it!" Sophia was very, very

angry as we rode onto the road again. "They didn't even slow down!"

"No, they didn't – you're right. I was really frightened there! But I wonder where they are going? They looked like cattle transporters?"

"I suppose they're going to Fredrik's dad. Where else? He has a business with cattle and all that, hasn't he? He's a businessman, isn't he?" Sophia was still very hot under the collar.

"Perhaps you're right," I said and patted Fandango's neck to show him all was well. "Perhaps he'll have cattle here as well, just like on his other farm?"

"Probably. But I want to ride home – now, or Alexandra will leave without me! Some friends of hers are also coming along, among them a boy called – "

What was his name? If you had asked me five minutes later, I would not have been able to tell you! Because while I half-listened to Sophia droning on and on, my thoughts were preoccupied with what had just happened. The trucks rushing past us had sent cold shivers down my back – and I couldn't understand why. It was no secret that Frank Carlson bred cattle for meat, and that a couple of trucks – maybe with youngsters behind the wheel – drive like mad on a graveled road, is not all that strange either.

Not long ago, our local paper had a story about how well Frank Carlson's animals were looked after on his farm. They wandered freely around outside, they had a large, airy, and comfortable shelter, and they had plenty enough to eat and drink, living a safe and natural life.

I was suddenly shaken out of my thoughts by Fandango, who stopped very abruptly, turned his head quickly, looking back to where we had come from.

Camigo did exactly the same – in fact, he turned so sudden and sharply that he nearly threw Sophia off!

"Whatever are the horses up to now?" asked Sophia, slightly worried, straightening herself in the saddle again. "If the trucks are coming back, we'd better jump into the ditch again!"

Both horses stood stock-still, tense as violin strings, heads lifted, ears pricked straight up. I stroked Fandango's neck and talked quietly to him, but it was obvious he took no notice of me. The horses had clearly heard something we hadn't.

The next moment a long-legged horse, a bay, with a white mane and white tail, came towards us in full gallop on the road. It was foaming round the mouth, dripping with sweat, and the eyes said it all; the horse was terrified!

It stopped dead the moment it saw us, neighed furiously and looked at us with wild, terrified eyes. It snorted, throwing its head from side to side, took a couple of steps towards us, hesitated, and turned sharply, jumped the ditch and disappeared among the trees.

"Did you see that!" asked Sophia, breathless, as if I could possibly have missed it. "A horse! Where did that come from? I never saw it before!"

"I have no idea," I said, and as I said it, I realized why those two trucks had sent cold shivers go down my spine.

A few seconds after they had thundered past us, I had heard a most terrifying scream mixed in with the roar of the engines.

Chapter 4

Sophia and I dug our heels into the horses and galloped over to the place where the horse had disappeared into the forest. But of course we didn't see or find it – the horse had long gone. The only evidence that there had ever been a horse there were the hoof marks in the soft gravel on the road. You could clearly see that the horse had been galloping flat out, stopped dead, taken a couple of steps, and then simply leapt into space across the ditch – and disappeared. There was no trace of it off the road, the ground was covered in moss and a layer of pine needles, so we had no idea which way it had gone.

"But where did it *come* from?" asked Sophia confused, looking around. "And where did it go to? It can't simply disappear in thin air!"

"I've got it!" I shouted. "Those two trucks must have been carrying horses and, when they unloaded them near that building, one of them ran away!"

Sophia looked at me – and it dawned on her.

"Come on!" I said, "let's ride back there again. I want to find out what's really going on!"

"OK," agreed Sophia, surprisingly willingly, and we trotted back the same way as we had come.

We hadn't gone far before we suddenly heard the roar of engines again, and we quickly led the horses down into the ditch and into the forest. Sophia was behind me, encouraging Camigo to follow. We were lucky, just as we got away in among the trees, the two trucks came tearing down the graveled road at a frightening speed, leaving behind a cloud of dust, sand, and diesel fumes.

"What are you doing now?" asked Sophia, Camigo had once more nearly thrown her out of her saddle. "Where are you going now?"

"If we want to see what they are doing, perhaps we ought to hide," I said quickly. "The machinery building is just over there!"

"Good idea!" said Sophia.

The ground was bumpy and very uneven, full of large stones, fallen trees, twigs, and undergrowth. The ponies felt their way, slowly – I was glad that both Fandango and Camigo were strong and sturdy.

We arrived at the edge of the forest quite suddenly, with the large graveled area and the building for machinery in front of us. But now, everything was dead silent. Not a soul to be seen, not a noise to be heard. Silence all around, with doors and windows shut. And no trucks. Nothing.

"How odd!" whispered Sophia.

I nodded. "Yes, it is. Shall we wait a bit and see if something happens?"

Sophia squirmed and looked uncertain. She wanted to go for a swim, but she was just as curious as I was as to find out what it was all about and what the building was that Fredrik's dad called the "machinery building."

"I think we ought to ride back home," she said after a little while. "We can come back here another day and see what's happening."

I agreed. It was getting close to eleven in the morning, it was already very hot, and both ponies were irritated by the swarms of flies and gadflies.

We turned and rode back the same way through the forest, and followed the graveled road and turned onto the track leading to our house. The ponies were very willing to head for home, trotting energetically in spite of the heat, in an attempt to avoid the winged pests.

All four of us were dripping with perspiration when we finally arrived back home, but it didn't seem to bother Sophia that Camigo was just as hot and sticky as she was.

"There you are," she said as she jumped off, removed the saddle and gave Camigo a friendly slap on his neck, "off to the paddock and have a good roll on the ground!"

"Hey – aren't you going to sponge him down with some lukewarm water at least?" I asked her.

Sophia shook her head.

"No! No time! I'm in a great hurry – you know I'm late! Can't you do it for me, please? You don't have anything going on today, do you? Other than clearing out that dirty old cowshed, right?"

I made a face at her. "Do you always have to be so lazy? You only think of yourself!"

"What's up with you?!" hissed Sophia. "I am meeting Alexandra; you knew that before we set out!"

"It was your idea from the start that we should ride over there, wasn't it?" I replied angrily. "There was no need for you to take a ride at all today."

"It was you who found that road, and ..."

"Girls! Girls! What's all this noise about?" said Mike as he came out from the old cowshed, a hammer in one hand.

34

He was probably helping Dad with something, and I was embarrassed that he had heard Sophia and I squabble like two little girls.

"Sophia doesn't want to sponge down Camigo. After all, he is dripping with sweat," I explained to Mike. "She's always so lazy."

"I am off to go swimming," said Sophia, looking at Mike with her sweetest smile. "Would be kind enough to sponge him down for me?"

"Of course!" said Mike, falling for her smile and taking Camigo's reins. "Off you go!"

"Thanks!" said Sophia, winking flirtatiously to Mike. "I'll help you some other time!" She turned to me and poked her tongue out, and walked with long strides towards the house.

"Why did you fall for that sweet smile of hers?" I asked Mike. "You're too kind, and she's too lazy, always avoiding anything resembling work!"

"Ah, so what?" laughed Mike and took the bridle off Camigo. "It doesn't take long to sponge him down. I'll just put his halter on and...."

At that very moment Camigo noticed that he was loose and free! Mike had taken the bridle off him only seconds before, and the halter was still lying on the bench by the stables. Camigo shook his head purposefully, and I immediately realized what was about to happen. Quick as a flash I threw myself forward to get a hold of Camigo's mane, but too late! He shot off like a rocket, giving me a push, which made me lose my footings, stumbling and hitting Mike – and letting go of Fandango's lead rope! The next moment both ponies bolted out from the yard, across the graveled road – and straight into Hans' oat field!

"NO!" I shouted. "NO! This can't be happening!"

Mike laughed and put an arm round my shoulders.

"Take it easy! We'll soon get them in again."

I shook my head. "No, we won't! They are impossible to catch once they are loose."

"Don't worry, let's get a bucket of oats," said Mike, obviously not knowing my ponies' sense of humor.

"What? When they are standing in a big field full of nearly ripe oats?" I asked and couldn't help raising my eyebrows.

"Just relax!" said Mike. "Get two buckets!"

I ran into the stables while Mike kept an eye on the ponies. I could see them through the window as I threw some oats into a bucket and shuddered. Fandango caught up with Camigo, and they behaved like two young foals in the field of oats; leaping, kicking with their hind legs, nodding with their heads, making an awful noise – and flattening the oats like tanks! Hans would go absolutely insane when he discovered it, and I trembled just thinking about it; I knew how furious he could be.

I ran out with the bucket and handed it to Mike, and both of us walked gently and cautiously toward the two ponies that had finished their romping and were now standing still, eating oats for all they were worth.

Fandango was the nearest one. He realized that his liberty would undoubtedly be short-lived; what was important now was to gobble up as much oats as in any way possible in the shortest possible time! He looked utterly peaceful and unconcerned, standing in what he surely regarded as a huge trough of delicacies, munching happily away, but I could see him keeping a careful eye on me and, just as I put my hand out to grab his lead rope, he shot up and sideways away. I swear he laughed at me!

"Darned pony!" I shouted angrily. Mike looked disapprovingly at me.

"Do you think you'll ever catch him if you shout like that?" he asked. "You have to entice him towards you, and you'll never do that if you're angry."

I stared furiously at Mike, but didn't say anything. He clearly regarded it all as a bit of a joke, but I was very worried. Partly that the ponies might stuff themselves too much and partly because I knew that Hans would blow his top if he discovered our two ponies in his field of oats!

"Look!" said Mike and laughed, walking slowly towards Camigo. "This is the way to do it!"

He waved the bucket temptingly, talking quietly to Camigo who lifted his head and looked at him with some interest with his dark, beautiful eyes. He even took a couple of steps towards Mike, snorted and pricked his ears up.

"Good boy!" said Mike gently. "Good boy! Come on now and into the stables."

He stretched his hand slowly out toward Camigo, who stood quite still and looked very angelic. I was just about to congratulate Mike when Camigo turned sharply and suddenly and ploughed his way further into the field, kicking his hind legs high into the air as if to say, "Catch me!"

Of course Fandango saw it all, and of course he had to follow Camigo. The two of them skipped and ran a bit further, before they stopped and began to eat from the abundance surrounding them.

"Oh man!" muttered Mike, and I couldn't help but look at him in an accusatory way.

"Don't show him you're angry," I said. "You'll never catch him if you're angry!"

"Oh, shush!" snorted Mike.

We walked after the horses. They moved slowly, stopping only now and then, taking a mouthful.

"It's no good!" I sighed, wiping the sweat off my forehead. "We'll never catch them! They'll be eating until they die from colic..."

"Cheer up!" said Mike, who had calmed down again quite quickly. "We'll catch them, sooner or later."

"I know – LATER!" I said gloomily. "And in the meantime Hans might well come along with his hunting rifle and shoot them both before we have managed that!"

Gradually we succeeded in getting the ponies to move in a homeward direction, and not toward Hans and Maggie's farm.

Mike was silent and determined, as was I, but inside I cursed the two darned animals. It was far from an enjoyable experience wading through all those oats, flattening it as we went. My throat felt parched from thirst, I was soaked through from sweat – and flies and other unpleasant insects were swarming round us like, well, like flies. And the sun shone hot from a cloudless sky.

At last, and it seemed like a very, very long time, the ponies came onto the road. At that exact moment – what happened? The very thing that shouldn't happen; two cars came along the road, whirling up a cloud of dust behind them. Hans was in the first car, while Fredrik was in the second, which was towing a horsebox, with his mom and dad!

"I don't believe it!" I said and gripped Mike's arm. "See who's coming!"

"Good!" he said and looked as if he meant it. "Then we might get some help." With that he walked briskly towards the two cars, which had stopped at the entry to our house.

I turned towards the ponies that were now quietly nibbling grass along the roadside and looked as though they never knew what a field of oats looked like. I was desperate, I was sure they would both be ill after all this gorging.

And I was far from looking forward to what Hans would say – I preferred not even to think of it.

I walked slowly towards them. Mike was talking to Hans and to Fredrik's dad, neither of them my favorite at the moment, and when the three of them saw me and came towards me. I wish the ground would open and swallow me, right then and there.

"You were lucky!" said Hans gruffly to me, knowing full well how bad tempered and angry he could be. I just nodded and looked down.

"Michael said it was all his fault, and had nothing to do with you, since he let them go, so –"

He cleared his throat and took his snuffbox out of his pocket.

"I'll try and get them," said Fredrik's dad and walked towards Fandango in a determined manner.

He talked softly to my crafty pony, who looked at him with some interest, chewing slowly.

Suddenly Buzy Bee neighed in his horsebox, and Fandango came onto the road to see who or where this other horse was. Fredrik's dad was quick and grabbed the lead rope.

"I've got you, you ruffian!" he said loudly.

Fandango looked a bit surprised at first, but then he followed him meekly over to me. Fredrik's dad handed me the lead rope, and Fandango gave me a gentle push with his nose, like he always does when he wants to say sorry.

I said, "Thank you," and led Fandango towards the stables. Camigo would undoubtedly have preferred to remain where he was, but suddenly decided that he was fed up with playing, and not wanting to be on his own he ran fast past us and straight into the stables and his own box. So when I arrived with Fandango, Camigo stood there, looking the incarnation of innocence asking, "Where have you two been?"

I stayed with Fandango in his box until I felt I really had to go out again. I found quite a crowd in the yard; Dad, Mom, Fredrik and his parents, Hans, Mike, and Sophia. She had come straight from the shower, her hair still wet. I looked at her with surprise; I thought she had gone for a swim a long time ago. But I suppose the fact that Fredrik had arrived made her change her mind.

They were all standing by the wooden fence around the winter paddock, looking at Buzy Bee, rushing round, tail high. He is dark brown with a white blaze and white, with short "socks" on all his legs. I had to admit that Buzy Bee was a very attractive pony, or I wouldn't have wanted him. Somehow he always gave me the distinct impression that he was not totally reliable, and I knew he was both fiery and difficult to ride.

"Do you have a horse or pony to keep Buzy Bee company?" asked Fredrik's mom in her sharp and slightly arrogant voice and Dad nodded.

"Yes, he'll be with old Maverick. Maverick is nice and placid."

"Good," said Fredrik's dad and looked at me. I realized he had just recognized me as the one he had met a few hours ago near his new machinery building – or whatever it was – and he didn't look all that pleased about his discovery. Which I thought was rather odd, since Sophia and I had hardly done anything!

Fredrik and his mom rolled a large horsebox into the stables. It was a big box of sheet metal – the kind you can even hang the saddle in. I wish I had one! I had wanted one for ages and ages, but they cost an awful lot of money, so the chances that I would ever get one were nil.

Dad and Sophia went into the stables to get Maverick, Mom went to make some coffee, and Hans jumped into his car and drove home – with Mike – leaving me with Fredrik's dad.

"Do you know what?" he said suddenly in a low voice, leaning forward, toward me.

"No," I replied, a bit surprised. "What?"

"I think you and your sister shouldn't ride in the forest near the machinery building. My truck drivers said they nearly ran you down since you were riding in the middle of the road. I don't want any accidents!"

I looked at him. There had certainly been enough room for both us, and the trucks on that road – if only they hadn't been in such a hurry, not looking and not slowing down.

"But –" I started, and before I could say any more, Fredrik's dad silenced me with his glare. He was far from as friendly and relaxed as he had been when we met earlier that day.

"That road is on my property, and I don't want a lot of young girls riding ponies up and down there. Keep away in the future – do you understand?"

I swallowed and nodded.

"Of course. The forest is big," I said, trying to sound casual, shrugging my shoulders. But his voice made me feel very uneasy, nearly afraid – but it also made me more curious than ever!

What was he trying to hide? And that terrified horse we had seen, where did it come from? I wished I had the courage to ask him, right to his face. Even if I had, I doubt I would have gotten an answer.

Just then the others came out from the stables, which was a relief. Mom came out and asked if anyone wanted coffee, but fortunately Fredrik's mom declined.

41

Instead, Dad let Maverick in to Buzy Bee. It went very well; the two geldings sniffed each other for a little while before starting to graze, side by side as if they had known each other for years. And five minutes later, Fredrik and his parents disappeared in as big a cloud of dust as the one they had arrived in.

"Whoa – what a day!" I sighed, walking towards the house with Mom and Dad. Sophia was already on her way to Alexandra's house on her bike.

"Quite!" said Mom, looking sternly at me. "How on earth did the ponies manage to escape into the field of oats? You really must keep them under control, Sara!"

"Michael was just about to put the halter on Camigo when Camigo shot away, and before I could do anything at all, Fandango rushed after him. It wasn't my fault," I said, defending myself with tight lips.

"That Michael kid –" started Dad.

"Stop it!" I said. "It wasn't his fault either!"

"No? Whose fault was it then?"

"Sophia's!" I snapped angrily.

"Oh?" said Mom. "If I remember correctly, she was in the shower then."

"Exactly!" I hissed. "Why don't you ask Sophia why she is so unbelievably lazy?"

With that I stormed up to my room and slammed the door behind me. There were times when I simply couldn't stand my parents – and this was one of them. UGH!

Chapter 5

I showered, and plunked myself onto the bed and read. I borrowed a good book from the library – a really thick novel. And since I wanted nothing to do with the world around me, what better to do with myself than read?

It must have been very good and exciting, because when Mom knocked on my door it was about two hours later. The knocking startled me.

"Is that you, Sophia?" I shouted.

It was Mom. And she looked worried.

"I think there's something wrong with Camigo," she said. "I think he is suffering from colic."

"Colic!" I shut the book with a bang and jumped onto the floor, following Mom down the stairs and over to the paddock. Dad had just let Camigo out through the gate, leaving Maverick and Fandango behind, both looking at us with pricked-up ears and great interest. No doubt they wondered why he was behaving in such a strange way. Camigo, that is – not Dad.

Dad tried to get Camigo to follow him, but Camigo did not want to move at all. Not a single step. Instead, he turned his head, looking at his swollen stomach, swishing his tail in a very irritated manner several times. Suddenly he started kicking against his stomach.

"I have phoned the vet," said Mom. "She'll be here as fast as she can." Dad nodded, and tugged gently on the lead rope. Camigo hesitated, and then took a few paces, very slowly. I took the rope from Dad, but Camigo did not seem to notice me at all. This surprised and disappointed me since he always greets me by pushing his soft nose against me. Now, he just stood still, head down, breathing heavily with a strange sound I had never heard before.

"Poor fellow!" I said, gently stroking his sweaty neck. "Come now, come on – you have to try and walk a bit. Just a little."

"I noticed that he started rolling himself on the ground," said Dad, joining me on the other side of Camigo. "I don't think he's been ill for long."

"What can it be?" I asked, trying not to sound as worried as I was.

Dad shrugged his shoulders.

"Difficult to say," he replied. "It might simply be that he ate far too much oats. Or it might be something quite different! There are several forms of colic, and they are not all due to the horse having eaten too much or too fast. People get funny tummies at times, as well."

I nodded, all three of us walking very slowly around the stable yard. I was glad Dad was on the other side of Camigo, because all Camigo wanted to do was to lie down. Every so often he turned his head towards his stomach and snapped as if to chase away whatever it was by biting it.

We managed another round or two; then Dad left to ring the vet again. Mom stayed with us, and we carried on walking, slowly. Every second seemed like a minute – where was the vet? It was an eternity since Mom rang!

I stroked Camigo gently along his neck. The sweat made his normally white coat look gray and dull. I wanted to burst out crying, seeing how he suffered. I felt so totally lost, not being able to help him in any way.

"You *have* to get better!" I whispered in his ear, as much to encourage him as myself. "You MUST –"

The lump in my throat would not go away, and I could feel my eyes filling with tears. I blinked rapidly a few times and wiped the tears away with the back of my hand. I had to be strong, not showing Camigo how worried I was! I knew how he could sense my feelings – so for his sake I had to keep calm!

We walked and walked. The sun was still blazing down from a clear, blue sky, and the air was still without the slightest wind. Dad was desperately trying to get hold of the vet on his phone, but all he got was an answering machine.

Suddenly Camigo fell over with a very heavy thud! I had no chance of preventing or stopping him, and I had to jump out of his way when he started rolling furiously from side to side, clearly in great pain.

"Get him up on his feet!" shouted Dad, rushing towards me. "Get him up!" That was easier said than done – Camigo was strong, and I nearly had to let go of the lead rope as he threw himself around.

Mom and Dad shouted at Camigo, who stopped and looked at them as if he suddenly realized they were there, and got awkwardly up, sighing loudly. He shook his coat, dust flying everywhere, and began stamping his hind legs frantically on the ground and kicking up against his stomach, all the time beating the air with his tail.

"You walk him a bit," said Mom uneasily to Dad. "Sara can't hold him, and they might both be injured if he decides to suddenly lie down again."

I shook my head angrily.

"No!" I said, "Camigo is my pony! I'll take care of him!"

"But Sara –" began Dad, but I interrupted him.

"You get hold of the vet – I'll handle this!"

I pulled the lead rope, and Camigo followed me, slowly, hesitatingly. I thought he seemed calmer and a bit more relaxed. He walked with his head down, but he didn't breathe as heavily and loudly as he had done a short while before.

I put my arms round his neck and gave him a hug. My little darling pony! I remembered all the happy and exciting times we had had together. Like the time when we won a very difficult and tight jump-off, with only a few tenths of a second separating us from the next competitor – who, I suddenly remembered, was Fredrik Carlson! And I thought of all the bareback rides during the summer months when we rode down to the beach for a swim or to the deserted farm, picking cherries. And our very first "Hubertus" hunt. I was so nervous I could hardly manage to sit upright, grasping his mane as if my life depended on it, right up to the first jump when it dawned on me that Camigo really enjoyed galloping with the other ponies— and it suddenly became great fun!

"Bloody vet!" exclaimed Dad, who for the umpteenth time had tried to ring the vet on his mobile, interrupting my thoughts.

"Did she say she would come straight here?" he asked Mom for the tenth time. Mom nodded.

"Yes, she said she would come straight away. But it's quite some way – you know very well how long it takes to get here from where she is."

"Yes – yes!" snapped Dad. "But for goodness sake, she could answer the bloody phone, couldn't she?" He shook the phone violently – you should think it was the phone's fault that the vet did not answer!

Camigo sighed heavily a few times as we walked slowly around and around, and I patted him on his neck again. Perhaps it was my imagination, but I thought he seemed just a little bit better; he walked a bit more willingly than only moments ago.

Suddenly a large jeep came up the drive and stopped near us in a cloud of dust, and a small, slim woman with a sharp nose and her blonde hair gathered in a bunch at the back jumped out. I took an instant dislike to her – don't ask me why, because I have no idea, I had never even seen her before. But my instinct proved to be correct – she was a really unpleasant person, totally different from our usual vet, Dr. Fransson, who was on vacation.

She walked towards us with quick, short steps, and without saying hello or introducing herself, she looked at Camigo.

"Is this the one?" she asked and, without waiting for an answer, she took the stethoscope, which she had round her neck, and put it in her ears.

"Yes," I started to explain, "he…"

"I'll listen to him first," she interrupted abruptly. "Then we can talk later." Without a friendly word or gesture to my poor pony, she took a step forward and pushed the stethoscope into Camigo's side. Camigo is normally a quiet and patient pony, but the sudden movement startled him, and he jumped sideways.

"Try and keep him still, will you?" snapped the vet to me. "How do you expect me to examine him if he's jumping around like a rabbit?"

"Good boy! Good boy!" I said, trying to calm down Camigo, who was looking very suspiciously at the vet. She took a step towards him again, without saying a word, and placed the end of the stethoscope against his tummy – only to make Camigo jump sideway again.

"For Pete's sake!" hissed the vet angrily. "Isn't there an adult here who can hold this pony still?" She glared at me.

"He's normally very good," said Mom, sounding friendly. "I suppose he doesn't like the stethoscope."

"Oh? But how else do you expect me to listen to him to find out what's wrong?" The vet talked to Mom the way you would talk to a naughty child.

"Let him smell it first – and stroke his neck," I said.

The vet frowned, but gave Camigo a few pats on his neck, and let him see and smell the stethoscope. After that, no trouble at all. Camigo stood quite still while the vet listened all around his stomach. Having finished, she took a step back and said:

"This pony is far too fat. Try and slim him down a bit, then he might not suffer any more colic in the future."

Dad, Mom, and I looked at her. Camigo might possibly be on the plump side (I'll admit that!), but fat? So fat that his health might suffer? Never!

"He escaped and got into a field full of oats," I explained. "He ate a lot."

The vet looked at me. "You'd better have a bridle on him in the future. You seem to have difficulties in keeping him under control," she said and put away the stethoscope.

I was speechless, although my brain was racing, trying to find a suitable reply. I didn't come up with anything, so I just stroked Camigo's neck. And this time he reacted – he bent his head, pushed his nose against me, rubbed me a few times, and then even tried to eat some grass from the edge of the yard!

"Don't let him eat anything!" shouted the vet, startling

48

Camigo so much that he lifted his head with a sharp and sudden movement.

"Keep him on the move – all the time," said the vet, and with a laugh I began walking Camigo again.

The vet took a syringe out from her bag, and filled it with a liquid.

I felt so relieved that not even that awful vet could dampen my joy!

"I'll give him something which will relieve his cramp," the vet said to Mom and Dad. "Bring the pony over here."

Camigo has never been afraid of syringes and injections and behaved beautifully. With that over, I continued walking him, while the vet was busy filling in lots of forms.

Suddenly Camigo lifted his tail – emptying what seemed half his stomach and intestines! I really don't know who was more relieved – Camigo or me.

"I didn't think it was serious," said the vet, slamming the tailgate of her car shut with a bang.

"Here's the bill and payment slip," she said. "Keep the receipt in case of complications."

Mom nodded, and Dad took the papers. The vet walked over to her car and opened the door. She was just about to get in when she hesitated, stopped – and turned to my parents.

"I'll just mention one thing," she said sarcastically. "There is no need to keep ringing me every two minutes when I have said I'm on my way."

"Well, no – yes," said Mom, taken aback by the outburst, "but we were so worried about him. He was very, very ill!"

The vet just looked at her.

"If I said I'm on my way, I'm on my way. If I have to stop and answer the cell phone every minute, it will only take longer."

"Yes...yes, well –" said Mom, lost for words, for it was Dad who had kept ringing.

"So remember that next time. My job is stressful enough as it is. I don't have the time nor the desire to sit chatting on the telephone with nervous pony owners all day long." She jumped into her car, slammed the door, started the engine, and disappeared with a roar down the road.

"What a terrible woman!" I could hardly find words. "She was so evil."

"We'll never have her back!" said Mom firmly. "I hope she is just standing in during the holidays."

Dad and I nodded in unison.

I patted Camigo and gave him a hug. "My little darling – I am so happy that you are better!"

"Keep walking him for a while yet," said Mom. "And keep an eye on him for the rest of the day."

I nodded. "Of course."

We walked around for a little while longer, and all afternoon and that evening I popped into the stables to have a look at Camigo at regular intervals. Fortunately, all seemed well, and when I looked in last thing at night, he was nearly asleep in his box, lower lip hanging loose and eyes half-closed.

Guess if I felt happy!

Chapter 6

The next day at breakfast, Dad suggested that Fandango and I should do some training jointly with Fredrik and Buzy Bee a bit later that day.

I was very much against the idea at first – I had no intention, ever, of riding with that nerd! But after some gentle persuasion I gave in. The trainer I normally had was abroad all summer, and it might do me good, I suppose, to have a different trainer and perhaps learn something new.

But when Mom peeped into my room a little later and reminded me of my riding lesson – just as I was in the middle of a very exciting chapter of the book, of course! I wished I had stuck to my guns. However, it was a bit late to change my mind, so I changed into my dove-blue riding breeches, put on a pretty and clean T-shirt, combed my hair and – just for once – gathered it into a neat bunch at the back. I certainly did not want to look like a slob, with Fredrik turning up looking like a professional!

"Your hair looks nice!" said Mom in a very appreciative voice as I walked through the kitchen on my way to the stables.

51

"Whatever," I said. "It's just that I'm fed up with it dangling in front of my eyes when I'm riding."

"You should cut it short," suggested Mom and washed her hands under the tap. She was busy with her flowers; there was perlite, soil, and cuttings all over and round the sink.

"No," I shook my head. "No, I don't want my hair shorter than it is now."

Dad came in, stern-faced.

"Hey – aren't you coming to the stables to take care of your pony? I brought him in so you can brush him down before you start your training. And don't forget your back protector today!"

"OK, OK," I said and drank a glass of juice in a hurry before I walked out to the hall and pulled on my riding boots. They were still covered in clay and soil from the weekend, so I grabbed some water and a kitchen towel and wiped them clean.

"WOW! What's all this about then, dressed up to kill?" asked Sophia sarcastically, suddenly appearing in the hallway. "All because Fredrik is coming over here to train, or what?"

"Shut up, will you?!" I snorted. "You know darn well I can't stand that snooty boy!"

"Hmmm," said Sophia dreamingly, "he may be – but he's a good horseman and he's cute enough to die for. If only I had time I'd stay home and watch, but I have to take off. See you!"

She hurried out the door, and I soon followed.

In the stables, I found Fandango half-asleep. But the moment he spotted me he lifted his head and neighed lazily, and I gave him a handful of hay before I got some brushes and a hoof-pick.

"You're not feeding him just before a training session, are you?" Dad suddenly appeared like a jack-in-the-box.

"Dad – I gave him about three straws, that's all! Stop it – I know he's a bit on the fat side just now, grazing all day, every day, but he still needs *something!*"

Dad muttered something – and left. I sighed with relief.

At that moment I heard a car arrive outside – it was Fredrik and his mom. Fredrik collected Buzy Bee from the paddock, and brushed him down outside the stables, while his mom was smoking a cigarette and chatting on her cell phone.

I led Fandango out from the stables just as Fredrik put the saddle on Buzy Bee, and the two ponies studied each other with interest.

Fredrik's mom was as elegantly dressed as last time, but she was far less ingratiating and friendly than the day before. Her voice was sharp and biting, confirming my feeling that I didn't like her.

I got Fandango ready and tightened the girth, and followed Fredrik toward our riding ground. Fredrik didn't utter a single word, he had just about, and rather reluctantly, managed a faint "Hi" when he saw me, so I decided it served no purpose trying to be friendly.

When we got to the riding arena, Fredrik looked disapprovingly around, and said in a rather surly voice: "What a small riding arena you have! And the jumps look like pieces of wreck!"

"Ride somewhere else then!" I hissed.

"There is nowhere else at the moment, or I would have!" He gave me a superior look and rode through the half-open gate.

"Have you ever though of *painting* this old rubbish?" he asked after having inspected the bars and jump supports Dad had put up.

"No," I replied, "we prefer the natural look!"

Just then a small, gray car arrived. I guessed it was our riding instructor. A thin, blonde woman in her 30s, dressed in beige riding breeches and a checked blouse, got out. She was so thin that her clothes seemed to hang free, with nothing underneath. And she had the most enormous nose I had ever seen.

She greeted Mom, Dad, and Fredrik's mom, and walked toward the riding ground. I noticed she was very bow-legged.

I took a deep breath, shortened Fandango's reins, and settled in the saddle.

The training could start!

But there would be no training, it seemed – at least not for Fandango and me.

"Do you mind? We are due to ride now. Please leave the riding ground, young lady!"

Fredrik's mom made a violent waving motion to me with her cell phone. I got off Fandango and walked across to her, Dad, and the riding instructor.

"But Dad said I could join in," I said, holding Fandango close.

"Good Heavens, no!" exclaimed Fredrik's mom and looked as if she had suddenly discovered something terrible in her soup. "Fredrik has private lessons with Ellie."

She hesitated, then added, "alone, nobody else," just in case I didn't quite understand what she said.

Dad laughed in that awkward, nervous way he always does when he's on a slippery slope.

"I thought it would be OK that Sara had instruction as well," he said quietly, and it suddenly dawned on me that he hadn't asked or mentioned it beforehand! Embarrassing!

"I would plefel to have only Fled on the liding glound,"

54

snuffled the instructor, looking important. "He can consentlate bettel that way." She quite clearly had enormous difficulty with her r's.

I couldn't help laughing and shrugged my shoulders.

"OK – I'll ride into the forest instead."

"But –" said Dad and frowned, "is it impossible for Sara to join in?"

"If she is –" said Fredrik's mom sharply and looked at me and Fandango in the same way as you look at something the cat had just brought in, "If she is, she'll have to ride when Fredrik is ready." Then she added, just to rub it in, "Fredrik is an unusually gifted rider, and the way Ellie instructs him is not suitable for everyone."

"Don't worry," I said icily and left the riding ground. "I'm not quite sure I can manage to keep up with Fredrik's level anyway, so I'll be off in the forest. Bye!"

"But –" said Dad. "Don't you want to jump, Sara?"

"If she's to jump and you want me to instluct hel," said the woman, trying to sound friendly, "I'm aflaid you'll have to pay for one extla lesson."

I found it hard to keep serious.

Dad and I looked at each other, and I shook my head.

"Thanks, but I know better ways to spend my pocket money," I said and turned Fandango and rode off.

Behind me I heard Fredrik's mom.

"What a snotty little girl!" she huffed. "Really unpleasant!"

"Mmm," said Dad.

Perhaps I should have felt miffed that I didn't get a chance to train, but to be frank: I felt more relieved than anything else. I had never heard of Ellie, and for all I knew she might be a superb instructor, but I was simply glad to get away from Fredrik and his mom. And boy – was it embarrassing that Dad hadn't asked or even mentioned anything about us training too! I decided to tell him outright that I wanted nothing whatsoever to do with Fredrik or his mom anymore. Nothing!

It was beautiful in the forest! The sun was shining, everything smelled of summer, and I enjoyed every second being out here with my horse, surrounded by nothing but nature. I patted Fandango's neck, and we both agreed that it didn't matter at all that we had to leave the boring, dusty riding ground behind!

We didn't go very far. Instead I tried to do some dressage with Fandango. We walked and trotted between the pines in a place where the ground is very even and soft. Now and then I stopped, and then started again, doing some leg yielding here and there. Fandango certainly didn't enjoy it at first, but gradually he relaxed and did very well. He behaved like he should behave, and obeyed my signals and commands. I thought it was much more fun doing dressage here in the forest than in the riding arena.

I had hoped that Fredrik, his mom, and his instructor would all be gone when I came back home again, but no. True, the cars had gone, strangely enough, but Fredrik was still trotting around on the riding ground. He looked bored to death, and I couldn't help grinning inside and wondered why his mom and the instructor had left the poor guy to remain here, with us.

I looked at the obstacles. There was one vertical and one oxer. Neither of them particularly high, and suddenly I got an idea! I shortened the reins, rode onto the ground and started a canter without as much as glancing in the direction of Fredrik and Buzy Bee.

Fandango understood immediately what I wanted to do,

and as I approached the first jump I could feel how he increased his pace, stretching and forcing himself as hard as he could. We flew over the oxer, I reined him in a bit, made a sharp right turn and jumped the upright with a good and clear margin.

Fredrik looked surly when I looked in his direction and laughed.

"I saved a lot of money there!" I said. I couldn't help being sarcastic.

"We jumped unusually low jumps today," said Fredrik, trying to be equally sarcastic, no doubt. "Buzy Bee can jump much higher than this."

"I'm sure," I said and shrugged my shoulders. "I think I'll take another round – it's fun!"

But before I could start, Fredrik rode across to one of the jumps, then dismounted and heightened both jumps a lot. Back in the saddle he turned Buzy Bee and jumped both jumps, quickly and without any effort.

"It's your turn," he said, sounding very pleased.

I shrugged my shoulders, shortened the reins and let Fandango canter one round before I headed for the oxen. Fandango loves jumping, and flew over it this time as well, but he was so excited when turning toward the upright that I had to sit right down in the saddle and hold him with all my might to prevent him rushing too fast and knocking down the bar with his front legs.

"OK," I said, holding Fandango. "I'll raise them this time."

I got off Fandango and increased the height of the upright, and then the oxer. I looked at the markings on the supports, which I had done a hundred times before, and put the top bar properly in position. Then I remounted Fandango, and reined him in. He began immediately to move his head and stamped his feet in sheer eagerness. In spite of the fact that it was very hot, and we were both perspiring heavily, he cantered towards the jumps at full speed – and before I knew what had happened we had cleared both of them!

I reined in Fandango and nodded to Fredrik, who immediately cantered towards the oxer. Buzy got the angle and distance wrong and started the jump much too close, but he was an experienced jumper and managed to extricate himself from the tricky situation and cleared the oxer – just. The upright gave him no problems at all, and Fredrik pulled him in a bit, rode to the jumps, and dismounted.

I let Fandango trot around, holding him tight, while Fredrik increased the height of the jumps once more. The oxer was impressively high, and I got butterflies in my stomach by just looking at it. The upright was already high, but now Fredrik made it even higher – higher than the oxer. I guessed he did so because he knew Fandango had a tendency to get too close to the upright before jumping, often knocking the bar off with his front legs.

This time it was Fredrik's turn to jump first. He looked a picture of concentration as he let Buzy Bee canter a couple of rounds in the arena before heading for the oxer. I could see that Buzy Bee was getting tired, but he was a plucky fellow, always doing his very best. Fredrik also drove him hard all the time. Buzy Bee jumped the oxer, hitting the rear bar, but it didn't fall off. The upright was no problem at all.

I swallowed and took a deep breath. How high it was! Very, very high! But I had no time to be nervous – not even to *think* about being nervous. All I knew was that I wanted to clear those two jumps more than anything else in the world!

Fandango seemed to have the same wish. I hardly had time to tell him to canter before he went flat out towards the oxer. And as we approached it at great speed, it rapidly dawned on me just how high it was. It really towered up in front of us. Fandango pulled hard on the bit, but I held back and we reached it in exactly the right position. Fandango took off, light as a bird. We seemed to float through the air for an eternity before we landed on the other side. It was much more like flying than jumping, and as we cantered away from the jump I realized that I had never before jumped as high as that with my pony!

I pulled on the reins, trying to slow Fandango down a bit. But he had tasted blood, and when we turned to face the upright, I became fully aware that I didn't have a chance to rein him in. He was too strong for me. I tried to make him slow down, but it didn't work. He rushed towards the jump like a beast possessed; it grew larger and larger and more threatening for each step he took. I tugged on the reins in a final attempt to slow him down, but it was too late. We were far too close. Fandango did his utmost and took off nearly vertically, but he didn't have a chance to clear the jump, and knocked off the top bar with his front legs, on the way up – just like he had done so many times before! I heard him hitting it, and I said a very quick and silent prayer that we might survive the inevitable crash landing.

It was a miracle that we landed softly on the other side, and I let Fandango canter to the end of the riding ground before I reined him in to a halt. I patted his neck, which was soaking wet with sweat, and whispered to him that he was the best and most clever pony in the whole world! It didn't seem to matter at all that he had knocked one down – he had jumped like he had never jumped before in his life, and when I looked at the oxer, I simply could not believe that we had jumped as high as that!

"Four faults!" said Fredrik curtly before pulling his riding helmet down and made Buzy Bee canter. I dismounted and put the bar back, and I had hardly time to move away before Fredrik and Buzy Bee came thundering towards the oxer. Buzy Bee was clearly tired, and he brushed against the top bar on both the oxer and the upright, but Fredrik was lucky. They did not fall off.

"I won," he said in his superior way and looked at me. "As always."

I looked at him, trying to keep calm, but seething with rage inside. I'll be dipped.

"One more round," I hissed. "Come on – one more! If you dare!"

Fredrik shook his head.

"No, thanks. Buzy is tired. And there's Mom."

He nodded towards the stable yard, where his mom had just turned in, and was getting out of her car.

Without saying another word he turned Buzy Bee and rode out of the riding arena, leaving Fandango and me behind. Fandango was still breathing heavily, nostrils wide open, and I patted his neck again and let him walk slowly round.

It was a pity that we had knocked that bar down I was so angry with myself that I had to grit my teeth. It was too late now, but I realized more and more that if I had left Fandango to do as he wanted, and not tried to tell him what I thought he ought to do, he would undoubtedly have cleared the jump.

I rode out from the ground with slack reins, and let Fandango trot freely over to the stables. The car was parked some distance away, but I could hear Fredrik talking to his mom. I know I get fed up with my parents at times, but I thought to myself that I would never swap them for Fredrik's! His mom talked to him in a sharp and nearly unfriendly way, and he didn't sound much better.

Fandango was dripping with sweat, but his eyes were sparkling; he was clearly elated that he had been able to jump nearly as much as he wanted to.

I removed my helmet, my hair was wet and stuck to my forehead, and I was dying for a cold drink. As soon as I had put the halter on Fandango and tied him to a post outside the stables, I put my head under the cold water tap in the stables, and drank and drank. It tasted heavenly!

I could see through the window that Fredrik and his mom were about to leave. Buzy Bee was in the paddock with Maverick, and he lied down and started rolling around on the dustiest spot. Like Fandango, he was dripping with perspiration, but Fredrik hadn't even bothered to sponge him down with some lukewarm water, in spite of the fact that his pony had been such a splendid jumper. No pat on the neck, no friendly words in his ears – no nothing.

Dad was talking to Fredrik's mom, and Fredrik just stood there, looking bored.

I dragged the hose out from the stables, but before I could begin to hose Fandango down, Fredrik spotted me and walked across. He grinned in a sarcastic way – I don't know how I stopped myself from hosing him down instead!

"Will you take part in the September Cup?" he asked.

I nodded. The riding club had always had a competition for ponies at the beginning of autumn, and I had put Fandango's name down for three of the classes.

"I'll win then as well," said Fredrik in a superior manner. "Just so you know! Buzy is a much better pony than that lump of lard you've got!"

"I don't agree with you!" I snapped, angrily.

"OK," said Fredrik. "We'll see!"

"Get lost!" I hissed and let some water hit his riding boots. "I don't know why you are always so cocky!"

Fredrik only laughed, turned, and walked away.

How *did* I stop myself from directing the water hose into his back?

I washed Fandango with lukewarm water. As usual, Fandango pretended not to enjoy it, I'm sure it is only a game, but I pretended not to notice; I wasn't in a particularly good mood.

I was going to show Fredrik – I certainly would! Fandango and I would simply *have* to win the next competition. If not, that unpleasant brat would probably laugh his head off. At our expense!

Chapter 7

The next day I decided to cycle down to the lake to have a swim. I phoned Mike and asked if he wanted to come along, but he couldn't; Hans had plenty of jobs waiting for him to do during the day. It was critical to get the new stables ready, since Hans would otherwise have nowhere for his horses in the fall. Mike was happy to work overtime, but I didn't think that much of it since it meant I had to do things on my own.

I found my swimsuit, and put it in a bag together with a clean towel, a magazine, which Sophia had left on the kitchen table, and a bottle of juice. Mom was kneeling by a flowerbed when I rode past, and she shouted something after me. I stopped and went back.

"There was an ad in the paper today about a horse," she said and pulled her gardening gloves off. "A mare, a thoroughbred-cross, 9 years old."

"Oh, yes?" It made me curious – and feel better. "And which stable is she in?"

"There are some private stables on the other side of the town, as you know, and she is obviously there for the summer. Do you want me to call them and find out some more? It might be worth having a look, at least."

"Yes, please," I said happily. "I'm riding down to the lake for a swim in the meantime."

"OK," said Mom, tending her roses. "See you later."

Whistling a happy tune, I let the bike roll freely along the gravel road leading down to the little lake. There is a little sandy cove there, which hardly anyone knows about, apart from us living nearby. Although I was still sulking that Mike had to work, I quickly began to feel better. It might just be that the horse advertised was the one I was after! I tried to guess what she looked like, undoubtedly she'd have long legs and be slim since she was half thoroughbred. And 9 years old – she would probably have jumped a lot, and possibly also done some dressage – a perfect background for a competition horse.

And with a bit of luck we might even be able to look at the horse that evening.

There wasn't a soul in sight when I came down to the lake. I quickly changed into my swimsuit and waded into the water. Absolute perfection! I waded further out, and swam round for a little while before wading up onto the beach again, lying down on the towel.

I just lay there, relaxing, while thinking of everything that had happened the last few days. The dark spot was most definitely my competition with Fredrik – the fact that he won irritated me to no end. "That jerk!" I thought.

I also thought of the horse Sophia and I had seen on the road in the forest some days ago. The terrified look in his eyes. Even though we only saw him a few brief seconds before he disappeared into the forest, there was no doubt in our mind that he was desperate. And I thought of how Fredrik's dad had turned nasty when he threatened us not to ride on that new road in the forest. What was it all about? What was the big machinery building for?

The heat made me thirsty, so I sat up to have some juice. Suddenly I felt goose bumps down my back – it was just as if someone was watching me! I turned round very quickly, but everything was as empty and quiet as it had been when I arrived. No one was there; I was the only one in the cove. The water made faint gurgling noises as it lapped the beach, and I could hear a motorboat far away. A couple of ducks swam lazily across the water in front of me.

It was nevertheless a bit eerie. I was alone, and yet I had the very distinct feeling that someone was looking at me. And when I heard the sound of a twig breaking, I nearly began to panic, and I swear my hair stood straight up!

Who could it be? What if it was a large elk? I remembered only too well how a hunter-friend of my parents only a couple of years before had to shoot an elk, which had turned aggressive and attacked people.

At that moment I spotted the horse, the very horse Sophia and I had seen in the forest! He came walking towards me, between the tall pine trees, slowly – looking apprehensively at me.

I got up, very slowly in order not to frighten him, and he was quite close to me before he hesitated and stopped. He studied me, carefully, as if he wanted to find out whether I was friend or foe.

Now, close up and with him standing still, I could see what he looked like. And he was not a pleasant sight! The worn nylon halter was far too small, and it had rubbed so much that he had large, bare patches on his beautiful head. His right eye was swollen and looked inflamed, and one of his front knees was swollen as if he had been kicked or beaten across the knee. He had large sores on the side of his hips – it looked as if he had been standing in a very tight space, rubbing against something. I also noticed something else; he had been branded on his hindquarters with the letter C and the number 377.

"Poor boy!" I whispered to the horse, who never took his large and beautiful eyes off me.

"Where do you come from, and who's been treating you that badly?"

The horse took a couple of steps towards me, and I couldn't resist stretching one arm out. He nosed the palm of my hand cautiously, and I felt instinctively that he asked for help! He tried to tell me something, I knew it, and I was just about to put my hand on his halter when he suddenly threw his head back and up, and he backed away from me.

He was frightened, staring at the narrow path that leads down to the beach, and then I heard what he had heard before me: laughter, shouting, and loud music. The horse looked at me for the last time, stiffened – and threw himself around and disappeared in between the trees. It all happened so quickly that I didn't have time to move or do anything; I was still standing there, staring after him, when a gang of young boys, about 10 or 12 years old, came on their bikes, talking and laughing, with the ghetto-blaster on full volume.

I cursed them inside me. I had been so close to the horse, more than just close; I had felt his warm breathing against my hand. And now – he was gone, within seconds. I wondered if I would ever see him again.

I picked up my belongings and cycled slowly home again. It was uphill all the way, and in the end I got off the bike and pushed it, so when I got home I was just as hot and sweaty as before I went for a swim!

Mom was on the veranda, reading a book about roses, which she closed the moment she spotted me.

"Ah, there you are, Sara! I got hold of the owner of the mare, and I think it might be worth having a look at the horse."

"OK," I said, for all my enthusiasm had evaporated. My mind was fully occupied, thinking about the poor horse I had seen on the beach – so much so that I had completely forgotten I had asked Mom to ring about the mare.

"And I promised Granny to stop in on the way with a couple of books, being it is not far from where the horse is."

"Is it OK that Mike comes along as well?" I asked.

"Of course. The girl who owns the horse will see us about 7 p.m. this evening, and then we go to Granny's on the way back and have a coffee. OK with you?"

"Yes, fine," I said, and opened the door to go in when she added:

"What's the matter, Sara? You seem so – so – far away?"

"It's nothing," I said. "Why?"

"I have a feeling that something is bothering you," said Mom and gave a friendly laugh. "Is everything OK between you and Mike?"

"Of course it is!" I said, getting irritated. "I just have a lot on my mind. That's not illegal, is it?"

"Sorry I asked!" said Mom and opened her book about roses again.

"Parents!" I mumbled and walked into the house.

They really can be annoying at times!

Mike appeared about 6:30 p.m. in order to come along and test-ride Chikita (the name of the mare), and that cheered me up a bit.

I had made my mind up in respect of three points. First, I would go down to the beach as often as I possibly could – it might just be that the horse would come back there again. I would take with me a lead rope every time, and a small bucket with some oats, and with a bit of luck I might be able to catch him.

Second, I would tell Mike all about it as soon as I got a chance to do so, with just the two of us present. And, third, I would ride over to the machinery building again and look more closely at it. I simply *had* to find out what Fredrik's dad was really doing – and why he had been so threatening a couple of days earlier.

At 6:45 p.m. all three of us jumped into the car to look at the horse. Mike sat in front next to Mom, and I sat in the back seat with a bag of books next to me on the seat.

"I thought we would stop by Granny's on the way back," said Mom to Mike as we turned onto the main road.

"That's fine with me," said Mike, without sounding too enthusiastic. He is quite shy really, and he hadn't met my Granny before.

My Granny's name is Anna. She is a rather small, but very determined lady living in a nice apartment on the outskirts of the town. She can be quite sharp, and when I was a little girl, I was a little afraid of her. However, now, I am able to look beyond and behind the stern outside, which is hiding a soft, kind person with a heart of gold.

Granny and Granddad divorced many years ago. Granddad is a happy-go-lucky man, and he has loved horses all his life. In spite of being nearly 70, he is now living on a small farm some miles from here – with his new wife Angela, her 13 Shetland ponies and a far-too-fat Norwegian Fjord pony called Buster.

But Granny, who can be quite sullen if she wants to, has

never accepted Angela, and if anyone as much as mentions Angela by name, Granny's lips go tight, and she glares at you. This is normally quickly followed by some sarcastic comments about how stupid Granddad is – in spite of the fact that its been over 15 years since they divorced, you would think she would have moved on by now.

It took only about 15 minutes to drive to the place where Chikita was. It is one of the town's largest private stables, and was easy to find because I had been competing there with Fandango several times – they have a very large competition arena with plenty of nice jumps.

A tall, blonde girl, dressed in riding gear, was talking to a couple of other girls outside the stables. She was very tall, nearly six feet, with long, blonde hair in a plait down her back, and large blue eyes. As soon as we parked the car she came across and shook hands with us all.

"I presume you have come to look at Chikita? She's in here. Follow me!"

We entered the stables, which were light and airy – and clearly very, very expensive! Mike whispered, "I wonder how much you have to pay to keep your horses here?" I whispered back that I didn't know, but I had heard rumors that it was very, very expensive.

Lovely stables! Airy, light, and the horses had large boxes, and it was so clean, and tidy everywhere that you could hardly smell the horses at all.

Chikita's box was at the far end of the passage, and I looked at her with great excitement – only to realize at once that she was not the horse for me.

She was sweet enough, in a way, but I didn't think much of her color, which was a wishy-washy light brown. And she was too slim in my opinion, with a long, very thin neck and a rather square back.

The owner had told Mom that Chikita was about 16 hands high to the withers, which seemed correct, but she had unusually high withers, so her back was considerably lower. Indeed, she was nearly saddle-backed, and I thought it would be difficult to find a saddle that would fit her. But she looked good-tempered, and the young girl sounded so expectantly hopeful when she asked if I wanted to test-ride her, that I said, "Yes."

A little later I sat on the mare, who was standing stock still outside the stables. I adjusted the stirrup strap and walked her towards the riding arena. Chikita walked at a steady and leisurely pace, and ignored all my attempts to make her speed up a bit. She couldn't care less about what I told her to do and, quite frankly, I couldn't be bothered to argue too much with her!

She behaved a bit better once we were in the arena, and I tried both trotting and cantering. She walked nicely on both reins, and she did exactly what I asked her to do – no more, no less. Her owner came and set up a jump, about 3 feet high, and Chikita sailed nicely over it. She didn't refuse – but she wasn't all that eager either.

On the way back to the stables we passed a meadow where a large, long-legged light brown gelding was grazing. He lifted his head and neighed contently to Chikita, and Chikita's owner laughed.

"That's Chikita's son, Cherokee. He's only 3 years old, but nearly 17 hands. I'll break him in this autumn."

"Goodness!" said Mom, clearly impressed. "How odd that such a small mare got such a big foal."

"I found the largest stallion I could find for a Dad!" said the owner and laughed.

Back in the stables we chatted for a while, and we said we would let her know the next day about Chikita.

Chikita's owner hinted – like people always do when you test-ride their horses – that quite a few had shown interest, so if we wanted to buy her, we'd better not wait too long. And, we promised, in spite of the fact that I had already made up my mind that I did not want her horse. Chikita was undoubtedly a splendid horse in many ways, but she did not suit my requirements.

We said good-bye, got in the car, and headed for Granny's apartment on the outskirts of the town.

"That's the most uninteresting horse I've seen for a long while!" snorted Mike as we drove away. "Completely sparkless!"

"Yes," I agreed. "I'm not buying that one!"

Mom nodded.

"But she had a beautiful head," she said, "and she appeared to be very calm and good-tempered."

"But I want a competition horse, Mom!" I said. "One with some temperament and fire in his belly – one with personality!"

"Yes, and one that costs a fortune!" said Mom and sighed.

"I don't think it has to cost a fortune," I said. "One day I'll find my horse, and then I'll *know* it is the right one."

Mom nodded, but I could see that she thought I didn't have a clue what I was talking about.

Shortly afterwards we parked outside Granny's apartment. As we went up in the lift, Mom stressed: "Please remember *NOT* to ask or say anything about Angela or Granddad!"

Mike and I looked at each other, and Mike nodded seriously. He had never met my Granny before, but I had told him what she was like, and Mike was clearly nervous. He is always nervous and very shy when he is meeting someone for the first time – quite different from the impression he normally gives!

And when Mike is shy, his brain seems to spin around with him. As it did this time; when my rather brusque Granny opened the door, her gray hair very neat and tidy, and with exactly the right amount of lipstick and immaculately dressed, Mike stretched his hand out and said cheerfully:

"Good evening, Angela. I am Mike!"

My Granny's reaction was – well, it could have been far worse! Her smile froze and her eyes narrowed a bit, and her voice was rather icy when she said:

"My name is Anna, but welcome anyway."

Poor Mike!

Rarely have I felt as sorry for him as I did just then! And rarely have I struggled so hard to keep a straight face as I did just then. How I stopped myself from giggling like mad, I don't know. But I did.

We entered the flat, with Granny hopping in front of us. Yes, she hopped. Her right leg was bandaged, and she had to use crutches.

"What on earth have you done?" asked Mom, concerned, "Why didn't you phone and tell us?"

"Oh – it's nothing! I was getting down from a chair and stepped a bit awkwardly, that's all. No point in making a fuss of a sprained ankle or whatever it is. I'll be fine soon."

"But surely you could have *told* us!" said Mom. "Do you need some help? What about shopping, for example?"

Granny snorted.

"I am managing perfectly well, thank you. Now, who would like something to drink?"

We all did, and before long we were all seated in her living room. It was very neat, tidy, and clean everywhere –

Granny is a bit of a stickler for tidiness. There were photographs of the many and various family members except one – Granddad, of course – on her sideboard. There was one of Dad as a baby, and when he was a student, one of him and Mom at their wedding, one of me and Fandango clearing a jump, and one of Sophia as a little girl, sitting on the steps in front of our house with a kitten in her lap.

Granny and Mom talked about a variety of things while Mike and I just listened. Granny's cakes were very tasty – and homemade, of course.

After a little while it did turn out that Granny really needed – and would like – some help. Her fridge was nearly empty, and if Mom would be kind enough to go down and buy a few items, she would appreciate it. But only if it was no trouble, understand?

Mom nodded and got up, immediately followed by Mike.

"I'll come along and carry," he said, nearly pleading. He was clearly relieved to be able to get away.

Mom took the hint and said, "Thank you." Granny made out a little shopping list, which – when it was ready – was not that little at all, and Mom and Mike left.

Granny smiled at me. "It's a nice boy you have found," she said. "You are very much in love – it shows!"

"Puleaz!" I said and felt I was blushing.

"How are things at home?" Granny asked. "With the horses, I mean."

I told her about the recent competition, and about our visit to look at Chikita a bit earlier that evening. Granny nodded. She was not all that interested in horses, really, but for Dad's sake she had taken an interest when he was younger and needed some help, both in going to the competitions and in the stables.

"And we are doing it all up," I continued. "Dad is converting the cowshed to stables, and we'll have the tack room in the old bricked part."

Granny looked at me and sighed.

"Your Dad – he does take on the craziest of projects." She straightened a couple of newspapers, which were at a slight angle in relation to the tablecloth, and continued, "It's hardly worth spending time or money on that rotten old thing. He should take it all down – not convert it!"

"I think it will be quite nice," I said, and Granny sighed again.

"Well, well –"

She stopped and looked up as Mom and Mike returned, and while Mom helped Granny unpack and put it all away in cupboards, drawers, and the fridge, I picked up one of the papers from the table and looked through it. It was an evening paper, mostly concerned with celebrities and sport, with a small news section.

Flicking slowly through it, a headline suddenly caught my eyes. It was on a page dealing with foreign news, and I would undoubtedly have missed it had it not been for the fact that it had a picture of a horse.

"Finnish competition horses stolen," it said. I read it quickly. It concerned a large stud for trotting horses where 10 horses had been stolen recently. Further investigations seemed to indicate that an organized gang had stolen them.

"Well, we're ready!" said Mom, putting the last carton of milk into the fridge.

"Granny – have you finished with this paper?" I asked. "If so, may I take it with me?" I held the paper up so Granny could see it.

"Of course, of course. What do you want a three-day old paper for?"

"I saw an interesting article," I said, "and would like to keep it."

Normally it did not take long to drive home from Granny's, but we had hardly started when we found ourselves at the end of what appeared to be a very, very long traffic jam. And it seemed particularly long for me; I just wanted to get back home and show Mike the article about the horses.

We moved slowly forward, stopped, waited, and moved slowly forward again. And so it went on. Finally we could see what the cause was, a white car had obviously gone off the road and was lying on its side in the ditch, and a large, red car was standing across the road, blocking half of it. We could clearly see skid marks on the road, and the white car had its side smashed in. A young man in jeans was standing next to the white car, talking on his cell phone, and an elderly couple was talking to what appeared to be the driver of a service vehicle, parked on the side of the road.

Just as we were going to drive past we were signaled by a policeman to stop, and a colleague of his, a bit further up the road, waved the oncoming traffic to move on.

Mom lowered the window and asked the policeman what had happened.

"There's been a car accident," he replied. The way he said it made it very clear that he thought it was a rather unnecessary question since we could see what it was all about. I wished Mom would be a bit more diplomatic at times!

"Oh, dear!" she said. "I do hope nobody is injured! I am a nurse, so if anyone needs any help."

The policeman shook his head.

"No," he said, "no one is seriously hurt."

"What caused the accident?" I asked. The policeman bent down and looked into the car to see who was talking; hesitated, and said quickly:

"The cars were traveling in opposite directions, and both drivers said that a horse suddenly bolted onto the road. They both had to swerve to miss the horse, but unfortunately they did not miss each other."

"A loose horse!?" I exclaimed. "What did it look like?"

"Look like? Why do you ask? Do you live nearby – and do you know anything about a missing horse?"

"No, no!" I said quickly. "I just wondered."

"We have horses," added Mom, "but our farm is some way from here, so it could not be one of ours."

Just then the policeman farther down the road signaled to "our" policeman that we could drive on, which we did.

"A stray horse?" wondered Mom. "Whose horse might that be?"

"Who knows?" I replied. "There's a horse in every second field along here."

Mom nodded. "True. And some people are very careless about their fences."

"Please!" said Mike. "Don't talk about fencing! Hans wants us to start preparing the new meadow on Monday – for his stallion Fireflight. And he wants a mighty high fence all round – a *wooden* fence!" he added with some feeling.

We continued to talk about Hans' horses' right until we turned into our yard. Mom had hardly stopped the car before I grabbed Mike's hand and pulled him towards the stables where I thought we would be alone so I could tell him my news.

Did I say alone? Smack bang in the center of the stables, who should be there other than Buzy Bee, tied to a post, with Fredrik putting a bandage on Buzy Bee's front legs. Maverick stood half-asleep in his box, and I felt sorry for him, having to be in here keeping Buzy Bee company instead of enjoying himself outside in the late summer evening.

"Why are you bandaging him?" asked Mike, obviously curious.

"I always bandage his legs the evening before a competition," replied Fredrik haughtily. "Many competition horses have brittle legs, and one can never be too careful."

"That may well be so," I said and nodded. I never used bandages on Fandango, but if Fredrik thought it was necessary – well, that was up to him, wasn't it?

I glanced at Mike, and we left Fredrik to it and walked towards the house.

"What is it?" Mike asked when we approached the verandah. "You look so secretive!"

"I am! And I want to talk to you about it. Come!"

We walked into the kitchen. It was empty. I listened to see if anyone might appear, but all was quiet, so I showed him the article. Then I told him about the horse which Sophia and I had seen.

Mike read the article and studied the photograph carefully. It showed a tall bay with long, nearly white mane and tail. The horse was looking proudly straight into the camera; he had a laurel wreath round his neck, and the driver standing next to him, holding the reins, was either making a face or crying from joy.

"Are you sure this is the horse?" Mike asked, and I nodded.

"The famous stallion Täthivalo is among the stolen horses," read Mike, out loud. Then he shook his head and brushed his hand through his short, blonde hair.

"I don't know – it really would be a bit odd if that famous horse should end up *here*, in our quiet backwater," he said. "I can't see."

"I know that, but – " I said eagerly, but Mike interrupted me.

"I know what you are going to say, Sara, and – OK, I'll come along. We may as well take a closer look at Fredrik's dad's machine hall, and try and find out what is going on. But I'll be very surprised if it isn't all above board."

"Great!" I said and smiled at Mike, who put his arms around me. It made me feel how much I loved him; he always seemed to understand exactly how I felt.

At that moment, Sophia came into the kitchen.

"Ooooh," she said, annoyed, pulling a face. "If it isn't the love birds." She made a snorting sound and grabbed the paper like a hungry child would grab food.

"Hey – what's this?" she shouted. "Finnish horses stolen?" She read the whole article and looked at me.

"You don't think – do you think this is the horse we saw?" she asked, and I nodded.

"Perhaps."

"We're going to try and find out what Fredrik's dad is *really* doing," said Mike. Sophia looked excitedly at him.

"I'll come along!" she said. "Let's go straight away!"

"Wow – not so fast, little Sis!" I said. "Slow down a bit –"

"Yes?" said Sophia. "You don't want me?" I could tell she was beginning to sulk.

"Don't be silly!" I told her. "We don't know *when* we are going or even *how*."

"Typical!" snapped Sophia, who had changed from being happy and excited to being hurt and upset in a matter of seconds. "Typical! You always leave me out whenever you're doing something exciting! Always! But don't forget

I was there, the same as you, that day, and I know just as much or as little about it."

"Sssssh!" I whispered. "Mom and Dad are coming!"

The front door squeaked open, and we could here Mom and Dad talking.

"If you don't let me come along I'll tell them all about it!" hissed Sophia and looked as if she meant it.

"OK, OK!" said Mike quickly. "On one condition!"

"What's that?" asked Sophia, looking skeptical.

"That you keep your mouth shut! SHUT! Not a single word to *anyone* – understand?"

"Cross my heart and hope to die!" said Sophia quickly, just as Mom came in.

"Ah – you're all here," she said and put her garden shears by the sink. "Fredrik and his mom just left."

"Yes, and Camigo and Fandango can spend the night out in the open," said Dad as he came in.

"What?" I asked. "Why? You know that Camigo will be big as a balloon if he's given the chance to eat all night."

"Well, yes – but Fredrik needed a box for his pony. They are competing tomorrow, they're driving nearly 15 miles, so he wanted his pony to have a peaceful night and a good sleep."

My first reaction was anger. Anger because Buzy Bee was in *our* stables. The agreement was that he could be in our paddock, *outside*, and *NOT* allowed to reside in Fandango's splendid, large box!

But then it suddenly struck me; this was a most unexpected and very welcome opportunity! With nobody home, we could look closer at that machinery hall of Fredrik's dad in peace and quiet. What a golden opportunity! And when my eyes met Mike's, it was clear we were thinking exactly along the same lines.

Chapter 8

I woke early the next morning. Yawning, I looked out the window and saw Fredrik's parents' car, with trailer, coming to a halt outside the stables.

I crawled back into bed, but it was impossible to sleep. Through the open window I could hear the sharp voice of Fredrik's mom, the clanking sound of the doors on the horsebox being opened, the bumps and thuds as Buzy Bee walked up the ramp and into the horsebox, the doors being shut, and finally the engine starting and the car driving off.

I wondered if they had let Maverick out, or whether he had been left in the stables. I really was too tired to go and have a look, but I pulled myself together, put on my sweater and shorts and walked downstairs. The clock in the hallway read 6:15 a.m., and with a big yawn I opened the door, peered against the bright sun, and walked across to the stables.

Maverick was in his box all right. He didn't seem upset or not at ease, but as I put his halter on and led him out, I talked quietly to him.

"Poor you," I said and patted his warm neck. "I think

they could have let you out instead of leaving you in here on your own."

Camigo and Fandango greeted Maverick, and before long they were grazing side by side. Fandango looked very pleased, having been allowed to spend the night in the paddock – he loves eating, and he looked full to the brim!

"You're hopeless!" I said to him. "I should really take you in now and keep you in there all day!"

But, of course, I didn't have the heart to do it. I left him in the paddock with the other two and went back to the stables again.

I thought that since I was up and about I might as well clean Maverick's box out. Having done that, I swept the stables floor and refilled the water trough in the paddock.

All completed I yawned, stretched – and walked back into the house. I am most definitely not an early bird, so I couldn't help feeling impressed with myself that I had cleaned out a box before 7 a.m.!

The house was quiet and peaceful – I guessed they were all still asleep. I went into the kitchen and grabbed an apple, and went to bed again and began to read my book. I was soon totally engrossed in it, so when Mom came and told me that breakfast was ready, I was surprised that it was already past 9 a.m.

Dad had finished his breakfast already and had gone out to carry on clearing the old cowshed. I sat down and took the morning paper – and nearly jumped out of my chair!

There, on the front page, was a large picture of the bay horse I had seen down by the lake. He was running on asphalt, with cars clearly visible in the background. The horse was heading straight at whoever took the picture, his eyes reflecting sheer terror. My throat went instantly and completely dry, and I had to swallow a couple of times.

"I think that's the horse which caused the traffic accident," said Mom, not noticing how shocked and surprised I was, as she poured me some juice.

"I wonder whose horse it is?" she went on. "I have never seen it before."

I shook my head, but didn't say anything. My throat was still dry and tight.

"It says there –" Mom nodded towards the paper, "that a driver who arrived there immediately after the accident managed to take a picture of the horse."

I read the article. It was quite short, merely describing the accident, adding that the police was seeking information about the horse.

"Well, I'll go outside," said Mom and finished her coffee. "When Sophia comes down, will you tell her I want to speak to her?"

"Oh, what about?" I asked, no doubt sounding as curious as I was.

Mom looked at me for a while before she said: "Never you mind – it is none of your business."

No sooner had Mom shut the door behind her, when Sophia stumbled noisily into the kitchen. She looked very tired, and yawned heavily a couple of times.

"Gosh – I never thought she would *ever* go out!" muttered my little sister and plunked herself down in a chair. "Am I hungry!"

"Mom wants to talk to you," I said. "What have you done this time?"

"Done? Me?" Sophia looked a picture of utter innocence. "I haven't done anything. I don't understand what you mean."

"Come on! Do you think I am stupid? You *look* guilty!" Which wasn't quite true, but it worked.

"OK, OK. Mom has found a few cigarette butts behind the stables, and she seems to think that I am puffing secretly away!"

"Oh – but she is right, isn't she?" I asked and laughed. "Who else would go behind the stables to have a smoke?"

Sophia snorted.

"It is not me! I promise!"

I was quite certain she was pulling a fast one, but I couldn't be bothered to argue with her, and I pushed the newspaper towards her.

"WOW!" gasped Sophia, and read the article aloud to herself.

"Look at the poor beast!" I said, pointing to the picture. "He's terrified out of his wits!"

"I'm not surprised," said Sophia, shaking her head. "Poor horse!" She looked at the picture awhile, then turned to me and said in a firm and determined voice: "We have to find out what Fredrik's dad is doing. And quickly! I'll bet anything it is something illegal with horses. Perhaps he is a *real* rustler!" she added, her eyes wide open.

"I don't think it is quite as bad as that," I said. "Let's not jump to conclusions."

Sophia nodded.

"But the more you have the more you want, you know! I'm sure he is a miser at heart! And don't forget that it was you who told me that he threatened you and told us to keep away from the place!"

"Uhmm, yes."

"If all is right and proper and his conscience is clear, why would he ask us to keep away?" said Sophia, sounding exactly like one of these clever detectives you read about in books.

Before I could say anything, Mom came into the kitchen.

Sophia clammed up immediately and went distinctly pale, looking equally distinctly embarrassed.

"Oh, there you are," said Mom. "Good!"

Sophia got up – moving quicker than she normally does. "I am off!" she said. "Alexandra and I are –"

"You're going nowhere!" said Mom sharply, and Sophia sank slowly down onto her chair again. She stared straight ahead, arms tightly across her chest.

"Well, what is it?" she asked. Mom held up a small, crushed cigarette pack.

"I found this one in your pocket yesterday when I was washing your shorts." Sophia looked at the crushed packet with a mixture of innocence and startled surprise, as if she had never seen it before in her life, let alone understands how it had got into her pocket.

Silence in the kitchen. I got up and put my glass by the sink, and wondered what Sophia would say in her defense.

"It's not mine. I was only holding it for someone, but put it in my pocket instead of handing it back," said Sophia quickly. Anyone – even Mom – could hear she was lying.

"You were holding an empty cigarette packet for someone, and put it in your pocket? Why didn't you just throw it in a waste paper bin instead?" asked Mom. Once more silence was complete in the kitchen.

Sophia looked very uncomfortable, so uncomfortable that I nearly began to feel sorry for her. True, it was her own stupid fault that she had ended up in this situation, but when Mom looked at you the way she now looked at my sister, you would rather she didn't. Much rather.

"Er... well...I just... "

Sophia tried to invent some sort of defense, but there wasn't much to say, really, and she suddenly decided that pleading guilty might be the best, and only, form for defense.

"OK – I'll admit it! It's mine! I have smoked a few cigarettes – so what? It's up to me what I do, isn't it?"

"NO!" said Mom – she was angry. "It is NOT! I don't
know how many times we have talked about it! I do not –
NOT – want you or Sara to start smoking. Is that clear?"

"I'll do as I please!" shouted Sophia and got up. "It's
none of your business!"

"It is all of my business!" said Mom, every bit as angry
as Sophia. I found it best to disappear, quickly. This was
going to be some battle, and I had no intention of getting
involved.

I lay down on my bed and tried to concentrate on my
book, doing my best to ignore the raised and heated voices
coming from the kitchen. After a few minutes I heard
Sophia scream something at the top of her voice, the
kitchen door was flung open, very audibly with some
force, only to be equally forcibly slammed again. Then I
heard Sophia storm upstairs and run into her room – slamming the door so hard behind her that the house shook.

Then silence. Only broken when my cell phone rang. It
was Mike.

"Hi!" he said. "What about taking a look over at
Fredrik's dad's place?"

"OK," I said. "But what about Sophia – do we want her
to come along?"

"We did promise her," said Mike. "She'll keep quiet, and
I think it is better that there are three of us." *Why* he didn't
say.

I sighed, and Mike said he would pick me up in 15 minutes.

I walked across the hall to Sophia's room to ask her to
get ready. I knocked on her door, and there was a long silence before I heard Sophia mutter a reluctant, "Come in."

Sophia sat on her bed, still looking furious. She had laid all her make-up in front of her, looking in a small mirror at the same time as she was glancing at some photos in a magazine, describing new and different ways of getting made over.

"We're going over to the machinery hall in 10 minutes," I said.

"Good!" she replied. "You do that!" She carried on brushing her long eyelashes with the mascara brush.

"But aren't you coming along?" I asked, and felt slightly relieved.

Sophia shrugged her shoulders.

"I don't care!" she said and grimaced. "Just get out and leave me alone!"

"But – " I said, and Sophia looked up.

"No, no – it's nothing," I said quickly.

"I suppose you think I've started smoking as well, don't you?" asked Sophia sarcastically and put down the mascara. "Yes, I smoke like a chimney every bloody day when no one is looking! There's a cigarette packet hidden in every single pocket in every single pair of jeans and trousers I have, and I spend all my pocket money on cigarettes. So now you know! And please shut the door when you leave!"

"Hello, little Sis," I said. "I know you and Alexandra smoked a cigarette or two behind the gym at school this spring, correct?"

Sophia mumbled something and nodded.

"Well, OK," she said. "But since then I haven't as much as looked at a cigarette. It wasn't my packet – I promise!" She looked at me, and I really felt she was telling the truth.

"But whose packet was it – and how did it get into your pocket?"

"Would you really like to know?"

I nodded. "Yes, of course."

"It was Fredrik's! He gave it to me in the stables yesterday, asking me to throw it away. I forgot it, and – well, Mom found it, as you know." She shrugged her shoulders again.

"Was she *really* angry?" I asked, and Sophia nodded.

"Was she! And I don't know how I can convince her."

"But why didn't you say it was Fredrik's? I am sure he can tell Mom that you are telling the truth."

Sophia looked at me as if I were off my rocker, and sighed.

"His parents don't know that he smokes, that's why he gave me the packet. And what's more – "

"Yes?" I said, as she hesitated and stopped. I was curious to hear the rest.

"He wrote his cell phone number inside the packet because we were probably going out one evening next week."

I could hardly believe my ears! "Are you mad?! He's – he's – he's not for you!"

"I think he's gorgeous!" said Sophia and gave a little laughter as if she knew something I didn't. "Drop-dead gorgeous! And great fun."

"Fun? Only when he wants to be!" I said. "Most of the time he is snooty and snobby, using people right, left, and center, and…"

"You only say that because he normally beats you whenever you two compete," said Sophia and laughed haughtily.

"Not at all!" I said, getting a bit annoyed with my sister. "If you really want to know – I normally beat *him*!"

"If you say so," said Sophia and shrugged her shoulders. "Whatever – I don't care. I don't want to come. In fact I couldn't care less about that machinery building! I have phoned Alexandra – I'm meeting her and we are doing something."

"OK," I said. "Have a nice time!"

"You bet I will!" she said, and that was the last I heard before I closed the door behind me and went to my room to get ready to go out with Mike.

Chapter 9

Mike and I drove in his little white car to the farm where Fredrik and his family lived. Being the road went round the forest, it took longer to drive than it did to ride straight through the forest.

The sun was shining, and it was hot and humid. Even with all the windows down it was very hot and uncomfortable in the car.

"I think it is going to thunder," said Mike, trying to find a decent music channel on the radio. The cassette player had given up a long time ago, but now and then – if you were lucky – you might just find a station playing some good music. And this was one of those lucky days – not only that; he found a station, which played two of my favorites, one after the other.

Mike turned onto the gravel road leading to the farm, and when we drove past the house it looked empty. No cars parked outside, and all windows and doors shut.

"Good!" I said to Mike. "No doubt they are all at the competition."

"Yes, but it is weird that you didn't see his dad this morning."

"Tsschh," I said and shrugged my shoulders. "I've met

89

them at numerous competitions, and they are always there, both of them. Fredrik is their only child, and they are following him around wherever he goes."

"You sound sarcastic," said Mike and laughed.

I nodded. "I hate him! He's not kind to his ponies, and you can't be more awful than that!"

"Mhm," nodded Mike in agreement, just as we passed the new gravel road leading to the machinery building.

"Aren't we taking that road?" I asked without thinking, and Mike shook his head.

"No. If we meet someone, we can't get away quickly enough. If we drive a bit further we can park the car on the side of the road so it looks as if we are just strolling in the woods."

"Park where?" I asked, looking round. The forest was dense and right up to the road.

"There's a little picnic place a bit further on," said Mike, and no sooner had he said it when I saw it; some sort of a tent with a camping table, a toilet, and a garbage bin.

"How did you know? Have you been here before?" I asked, and Mike nodded, very pleased with himself.

"I drove out here last night. This road is part of a tourist trail or something, that's why there are picnic places at certain intervals."

I couldn't help laughing. "Tourist trail? Here? I've never seen anything resembling a tourist on this road! Anyone wanting to play tourist would pick a more beautiful area than here, in the middle of a forest."

"Perhaps. But I read in a book Hans has that some very rare types of orchids are growing here. They like it damp and marshy, apparently."

"You're crazy!" I said as he parked the car, and gave him a quick kiss.

"I suppose that's why I like you," he grinned.

We locked the car and started to walk in the direction of the machinery building not far away.

We kept parallel to the road, walking between the trees, not to be spotted if someone should happen to drive or walk past. It was hot and sticky, and I got wet from sweat almost immediately. There was a lot of shrubbery, twigs, and rocks all over the place, making it difficult. Mosquitoes, black flies, and other such delightful things swarmed around us, and I wished I had put on jeans and a sweater with long sleeves. Shorts and a T-shirt were not much protection against aerial attacks.

"I have had more fun than this!" I puffed.

Mike nodded and smiled, "Yes, but we're nearly there." He pointed, and there – right in front of us – was the new road.

"Good!" I sighed. "Ouch!"

A sharp bite on my right leg, and this time I got him! A large horsefly. I rubbed my leg – it was hurting.

"Poor you," said Mike, full of sympathy, dressed in jeans and a long-sleeved T-shirt. "But why didn't you put on some more sensible clothes?"

"I don't know," I muttered.

We left the trees behind and walked along the new road, heading for our target.

We arrived at the large clearing, which seemed to be as devoid of people as Fredrik's house.

Nevertheless, we stood very still for a long time, listening, before we dared to go any further. It was a long and open stretch from the relative safety of the forest to the machinery building. I found it very uncomfortable walking across the large, open graveled area. We would have absolutely nowhere to hide if someone should happen to look out – and if they did, we would be spotted immediately. My heart was pounding so loudly from sheer fright, I was convinced it could be heard a long way away. I kept looking nervously around all the time, like a frightened animal. But all was quiet and empty.

It was eerie; the hot sun beating down; the silence was total – apart from the sound of the gravel being crushed under our feet as we walked light-footed and cautiously forward – not even the birds were singing. Mike squeezed my hand hard in silence – he was as nervous as I was.

The graveled area seemed to have been made for taking heavy machinery. But Fredrik's dad had obviously intended to have animals there as well, because before we reached the building we passed six small square enclosures, three on either side of a wide corridor formed by fencing. The corridor led to a couple of large, double doors at the rear of the building.

All the enclosures were strongly fenced in, with uprights and horizontals made from solid wood, and gates of welded iron pipes.

"Whatever do you think he's going to have here?" I asked, and noticed I was whispering.

"Don't know," replied Mike thoughtfully. "Cows, calves – whatever. Seems reasonable, doesn't it, bearing in mind what he's been doing so far?"

I know it sounds silly, but the closer we got to that large building, the more it felt as if it was something more and much meaner than just an ordinary and rather ugly building made from green, corrugated panels. When we finally reached the hot wall, the whole building seemed to loom over us in a threatening way, and I couldn't help wishing I had never thought of coming here, however curious I was.

There was a small, black door next to one of the double

doors, and Mike pulled the sleeve of his T-shirt down over one hand and tried the handle.

"You're crazy!" I whispered. I found it difficult to speak, my mouth was dry and my stomach was in a tight knot. "What if there's someone in there!"

"No, I don't think so," Mike whispered back.

"But what if they have a security alarm?" I was scared.

"If so, this door will be locked," said Mike, sounding calm and convincing. "You normally lock *and* have a security alarm – not one or the other."

Slowly, very, very slowly, Mike moved the handle down and opened the door. Very, very carefully, and only an inch or two, just so we could peep in.

We did – and both of us pulled back immediately. What a smell! I had never smelled anything so strongly unpleasant in all my life. My eyes were stinging and watering, and I had to blink several times before I could confirm what I thought I had seen in the semi-darkness; the whole building was full of horses!

The building was full of boxes, like the enclosures outside, but made from steel pipes, not wood. And each box held five or six horses, cramped together, side by side. Horses of every size, type, and description. Some were cold-blooded or warm-blooded trotters, but I also saw some Fjord horses and some smaller ponies.

The smell was terrible, and so was the heat. There appeared to be no ventilation of any sort, and the horses were apathetic and wet from perspiration, standing still, heads down, paying no attention to anything.

Long water troughs were placed by the boxes, but they were dry and empty. The horses had no bedding, for all I could see a few battered bits of straw in the nearest box, flattened and covered in horse droppings and urine.

Suddenly a large, dark horse spotted us. He lifted his head and neighed hopefully – as if he had hoped we had come to take him away from this terrible, awful place. I nearly started to cry as some of the others joined in, but suddenly Mike shut the door and grabbed my arm.

"Come! Hurry!" he said.

"What?" I began, but he put a hand over my mouth. We ran to the nearest trees as fast as we could and tumbled and stumbled in among the undergrowth.

"I heard something!" whispered Mike, just as the two green trucks roared in, whirling up a cloud of dust.

My heart was thumping away, loudly. I thought my chest was going to explode, and I was shaking all over.

Panting, we hid behind two large boulders, which had some bushes in front. We peeped cautiously between them to see what was happening, and I saw something I hope I will never, ever see again in my whole life!

One of the trucks backed right up to the double doors, which opened. From inside the building, we could hear the noise of the horses, neighing and stamping their feet in a frenzy. Seven horses came limping and staggering out of the truck. Seven large, heavy workhorses, all bays of various ages. The man unloading them shouted and screamed at the horses, and whipped them with a whip to make them move faster. He drove them into the building. As soon as the truck was empty, it drove off, leaving the space vacant for the next one.

And the same thing happened again, but now with very different horses. These looked like thoroughbreds or trotters, long legged and sleek. Like the first lot, they staggered and limped out of the truck. A beautiful bay with a yellow halter skidded, slipped, and fell down the ramp, and I had to bite my hand not to start crying and shout out loud when I saw the man hit her hard with the whip to make the horse get up again and follow the others into the stinking darkness.

With both trucks empty and all the horses inside the building, the four men stood outside the doors, chatting and smoking for a long time. They obviously didn't give the horses or surroundings a second thought, for all the noise was deafening; the horses neighing, stamping their feet, banging frantically against the walls. It was awful! But the men just stood there, smoking, talking, even laughing!

The last thing they did before driving away was to lock the little black door.

Mike put his arm round me, and we hugged each other for a long time. I started to cry, and I sensed that Mike was as unhappy as I was.

The noise from the building died gradually down, and soon it was as silent as when we arrived. But we knew that the building was full of thirsty, hungry, and terrified horses – and we couldn't lift a finger to help them!

"Let's break in and give them water at least!" I sobbed.

Mike shook his head.

"No, that's not a good idea," he said slowly. "But we have to try and stop this. We *must!*"

Chapter 10

I can hardly remember how we got back through the forest and to the car. The horseflies and mosquitoes were just as bloodthirsty as before, it was just as hot and sticky. We were both dripping wet with perspiration, and it was just as difficult to walk through the undergrowth and over the uneven ground as before; even so – all I could think about was those poor horses inside the large building behind us.

We were still silent as we got into the car. We did not listen to the radio on the way back – we just sat there, without saying a word.

It was not until we turned into our driveway that I broke the silence. "What shall we do now?" I asked.

"I don't know – I really don't know," said Mike. He sounded tired and depressed. "Perhaps," he added after a short pause, "perhaps we should call the police?"

I nodded in reply. We *had* to do something to help those poor horses, but we couldn't do it alone, that was impossible.

The house was quiet and empty, but Mike and I took the telephone into my room just in case someone should suddenly appear, and Mike rang the police. I left him to talk since I felt that if I had to describe the circumstances and what we had seen, I would start to cry.

The police answered quickly, and Mike described very briefly what we had seen in that building. Then he just listened a long time, now and then trying in vain to get a word in, getting visibly more and more upset.

"So you're not going to do anything about it?" he finally shouted. "Those horses are *dying* from mistreatment!"

I could hear the voice at the other end, but not what it said.

"But the horses need help *now*! They can't wait until Monday!" shouted Mike angrily, and slammed the receiver down. I had never seen him so furious!

"What did they say? Why won't they come?" I asked anxiously.

"Would you believe it!" snorted Mike. "She wrote down that the horses seem to be – *seemed to be* – mistreated, and that we would like to be anonymous. But would they drive out there and have a look? No!"

"But why not? Didn't she understand how serious it is?" The tears were welling up in my eyes.

Mike shook his head.

"Obviously not! They told me that the entire police force, which consists of only three officers, is on duty at a festival in a field outside the town this evening, so it has to be murder – at least – before they can spare someone to look into it."

"But the horses are *dying,*" I cried. "Mike – what shall we do – what *can* we do?"

"We'd better ring the vet," said Mike, looking round for the telephone book. "Do you know the number off-hand?"

I didn't, but got the telephone book. Mike looked up the number and called it.

"If it's that awful woman who came and looked at Camigo, I don't think we'll have much luck!" I said.

Mike listened, but said nothing. After a while he replaced the receiver.

"The vet is on vacation, and I was referred to the vet on duty at the animal hospital."

"Animal hospital! But that's about 20 miles away! I suppose you may as well call them and see." I sighed.

Mike did. But the only person he could speak to was one of the nurses, who, after Mike had explained what it was all about, referred him to the police. "This is a police matter," she said, "not one for us," although she could understand how upset we were.

When Mike finished the conversation, I walked across to the window and looked out. Fandango and Camigo were grazing happily – clean, fresh, green grass – and I thought of those poor and frightened horses in the boiling hot building, without water and food. The tears were streaming down my cheeks.

Mike put one arm round me; we stood there, silent, looking at the two ponies, no doubt thinking the same. After a while he carried the telephone out into the hallway again.

"I think we should go for a swim," he said quietly as he came back in.

"What?" I said, a bit startled. I stared at him. *Boys*! They could be very, very difficult to understand at times – and this was one of those times! We had just seen a whole lot of horses in unbelievable conditions, cooped up in a hot place without water or food, suffering – and all Mike could think about was to take a trip down to the beach and have a swim because HE was hot!

"I thought we might just happen to see that horse again, or at least find some tracks we could follow," said Mike quickly, as if he had read my thoughts.

I blushed slightly, and lowered my eyes. How *could* I have misjudged him that much! I hoped he hadn't noticed my reaction. That's what can happen if you jump to conclusions. At least I didn't say anything sarcastic or nasty to him – and it wasn't *Mike* I was annoyed at – it was the fact that nobody seemed to care the slightest about those horses suffering in agony.

A little later we cycled down to the bay, with our swimwear in a bag each. At the bottom of my bag I had a lead rope and some sugar cubes in a plastic bag. Neither of us really expected to see the horse – and the moment we got to the beach, we realized that the horse would be nowhere near the place.

The little beach was overflowing with rugs, sheets, picnic baskets, bicycles, and buckets and spades. And in between all this, space permitting, were moms and dads, little children playing or paddling at the water's edge, some boys were fishing from a rock, a couple of girls kicked a ball round on the strip of grass, and some older children ran around, splashing water on each other, shouting and screaming. A radio on full blast in the middle of it all added to the chaos.

Mike and I looked at each other.

"I thought you said it was always empty!" he said and laughed. "What's it like when it is full?" He smiled at me and grabbed my hand. "Now that we're here, we may as well go for a swim right?"

I did, and nodded. It was still hot, and I was sticky and sweaty.

It was a beautiful feeling, wading into the clear, cool water, swimming side by side with Mike into deeper water. There is a raft a bit out from the shore, anchored to the bottom of the lake by a chain. You can dive from it – or just lie there and enjoy the sunshine.

It was empty, so Mike and I hauled ourselves onto it. Everything around me was right – sunshine, a refreshing swim, and Mike next to me – but I had a lump in my throat all the time; I just couldn't get those poor horses out of my mind. In fact, the cool water and fresh air on my face only helped to underline the heat and awful conditions of the horses. I tried to tell myself that the men we had seen surely would return and give the horses some water, at least, but I had to admit it was probably mere wishful thinking.

Mike and I sat on the edge of the raft, feet splashing in the water. There was no wind, and the water was like a mirror. A couple of ducks took off not far from us, and we could hear the sound from an outboard motor, but couldn't see the boat. And the noise from the beach was a din in the background.

"Are you thinking what I am thinking?" asked Mike, and I nodded.

"Yes. You know, I would never have imagined that he could possibly be such an evil man, treating horses like that," I said. "How can he? I just don't understand it; Fredrik's competition ponies are treated like gold dust, wrapped in cotton."

"We have to call the police again when we get back," said Mike, taking my hand in his.

"Yes, or someone at the council who is in charge of the well-being of animals," I said. "Mom and Dad will know who to contact."

"Do you know what I think is the worst of it all?" asked Mike slowly.

"No?" I replied and looked at my toes in the water.

"That it won't really help much if we stop Fredrik's dad.

There'll always be someone, ready and willing to step in to make a quick buck from carrying animals long distances to wherever the meat prices are highest. It makes you wonder."

I looked at him. "So you think we shouldn't do anything, is that it?" I couldn't believe I had heard him correctly. "Do we just leave those poor horses to?"

He squeezed my hand. "No, Sara, don't be silly. Of course not!"

I smiled through tears. "Good! We have to try and stop him, whatever else we do," I said and squeezed his hand back really hard. "Even if saving these horses makes no real difference to the world, to these poor horses it means everything."

"I'm all with you," said Mike.

"Great!" I said and dived off the raft. I swam underwater for as long as I could before I had to surface and gasp for air. Mike was still standing on the raft, waving me towards him.

"What is it?" I shouted. He didn't reply, only waved frantically.

"WHAT IS IT?" I shouted again. He placed one finger over his mouth and shook his head.

I swam quickly to the raft and Mike pulled me out of the water.

"What?" I started, but Mike turned me round and pointed.

"Look over there!" he said. "Isn't that a horse over there?"

I peered against the bright sunshine reflected by the calm water, shading my eyes with one hand. Mike pointed to somewhere quite a way away. I was just going to tell him I couldn't see a horse when something moved. Mike was right – it *was* a horse. I could see the golden bay color in the sunlight, and the white mane seemed to flow freely in the air when the horse shook his head from side to side.

"It must be that bay!" I said. "But what's he doing over there? I can't see any paths or anything there, just bracken and thorns."

Mike shielded his eyes, peering at the other beach for a long time, not saying a word. I did the same, also in silence. Suddenly we heard a very faint sound – a desperate neighing from the horse, so far away!

"Do you think he is stuck in the water or something?" said Mike, sounding very anxious.

"Why do you think that?"

"If you look...see…it looks as if he's in the water, and not ashore. And he's throwing his head around in a strange way. If he had gone down to the water to drink, wouldn't he have finished by now?"

"We have to get over there!" I said and jumped into the water. "Come on!"

"But how?" asked Mike as we swam back to shore as fast as we could.

"I have no idea! I have never been over to that part. But I have a feeling we have to be quick!"

But it was easier said than done. When we got home, Dad had just finished washing the old cowshed with a high-pressure hose, and when he spotted Mike and me his face lit up.

"Hello, you two!" he smiled, waving the nozzle at us. "Any volunteers to take over here?"

"No," I said quickly. "We have to rush off somewhere!"

"What's up?" asked Dad, putting the nozzle down, looking curious. I looked at Mike, who gave me a quick and clear signal, which meant "Don't tell him!"

"We're off to buy a pizza," I said, and Dad's face lit up even more.

"Good! Buy some for the rest of us as well! I'd like a calzone special, with extra cheese, and Mom will undoubtedly have a–"

"But we won't be back for several hours; we're meeting some friends!" I could feel I was blushing; I really did not want to lie to my Dad like that.

Dad's face dropped.

"But couldn't you?"

"Dad – we're in a big hurry!" I interrupted. "You'll have to buy your own pizza if you want one. I'm sorry –we can buy some another day, but not now."

"Ah, well, if you say so," said Dad, going back into the cowshed.

Mike hurried home to get the car, and I dashed up to my room, threw my swimming gear into a corner and jumped into a pair of old jeans. I put on an old cotton shirt, socks, and gym shoes. I ran downstairs again as fast as I could and out the door, just as Mike arrived in his car. I jumped in before he had time to switch the engine off.

As we drove off, Dad appeared from the cowshed.

"I feel bad about your Dad," said Mike. "He's becoming quite friendly towards me – even though I work for Hans."

"Yes, I know. But he'll have to wait for his pizza until some other time. Do you know where we are going?"

Mike handed me a map of the area, and I put it on my lap. It wasn't a very detailed map, but some of the minor roads were at least marked, together with houses and farms.

It was easy to find our house, road, and our little beach on the map – it was not so easy to try and work out where we had seen the horse in relation to where we were and how to get there.

I could see a small road that I judged to be a mile or so from the spot where I thought the horse might be. But I wasn't sure about the exact spot, so I suggested to Mike that if he could find the lake, we could follow the edge of it until we found the horse – assuming it was still there, of course.

But the map and the terrain were not in harmony; the road was marked on the map as a fairly good gravel road, but when we found it, it turned out to be an old, overgrown road, probably used for transporting lumber years ago.

Mike drove into the forest as far as he could, but after only a couple of hundred yards there was no way for the car to get through. The shrubs and trees had taken over, so we had to abandon the car where it was, and start walking.

It was just as hot as it had been earlier, and the silence here in the forest was nearly total. I say "nearly," had it not been for the buzzing and humming of all the mosquitoes and horseflies, it would have been total. But when all these flying insects, no doubt happy in their undisturbed environment, spotted us, they got even happier and shouted out loud: "FOOD!"

We struggled along the overgrown road. Although I had the map in my hand, it wasn't of much help. The road ended by a turning area next to a clearing. According to the map, all we had to do was to cross the clearing, walk through the forest a short distance on the other side – and we would be at the lake. I am not an expert map-reader, but that's what it looked like. And neither of us had ever been in this part of the forest.

"Once we're down on the beach it will be easier," said Mike, encouraging us both as we struggled through the undergrowth.

The lumberjacks and machinery had left everything in a

mess when they departed all those many years ago. Tree roots; deep ruts made by heavy machines; some felled and half-rotted trees. Flowers and young trees and shrubs gave evidence that nobody had been here for a long, long time.

Mike had been sensible enough to bring a bottle of water along in his backpack, and rarely had water tasted as lovely as it did then.

"How far do you think it is?" Mike asked. I looked at the map.

"A couple of hundred yards," I said.

"Good!" He wiped his forehead with the back of his hand. "Let's keep going."

I nodded.

A few more steps and the forest thinned out a bit, making progress easier. We came across a small track that I guessed had been made by animals walking down to the lake to drink, and we followed it. I was right; It led us to the lake. Strangely enough there seemed to be far less blood-sucking insects there – perhaps they didn't like the little breeze which cooled our hot faces.

Mike and I hurried right down to the water's edge. The lake was still like a millpond, and on the other side, far away, we could see our little beach and the raft in the water. I also saw a large, dark cloud looming over the horizon – a thundercloud if ever I saw one. Which explained the hot, still air we had had all day.

But no horse in sight!

"We should be in the right place – more or less," I said, pointing to the crumbled map.

I showed Mike on the map the route we had followed, and he agreed.

"I think we have to go a bit more in that direction," he said, pointing.

"Yes, but – " I began, and was suddenly interrupted by a loud neighing, sounding much more like a scream.

I froze. The neighing came from somewhere near by, and yet, we couldn't see the horse calling for help! And one thing that was certain, it was a desperate cry for help!

Chapter 11

Mike grabbed my hand, and we ran as fast as we could along the edge of the lake in the direction we thought the neighing had come from. And the moment we rounded some large boulders, surrounded by shrubbery, we spotted the horse!

He was standing in the water, a few feet out, with a million horseflies and mosquitoes swarming all over and round him. He had lowered his head to just above the water, and we saw straight away that he was badly bitten by the insects. He still had his halter on – it had rubbed off even more hairs, and his head was splattered with bare, hairless patches. When he heard us, he lifted his head. One of his eyes was completely closed, with a yellowish, thick liquid running from it.

"Poor guy!" exclaimed Mike with feeling. "Poor guy!"

Mike quickly peeled off his backpack, opened it and took up the lead rope he too had wisely packed. He waded out to the horse, fixed the lead rope and tried to encourage the horse to walk towards dry land.

But however much the poor creature wanted to follow

Mike, he couldn't! His left hind leg was obviously stuck, so I waded out to Mike and took the lead rope in order to help him.

Mike waded around to the stuck left leg and felt carefully along and down it. The horse threw his head uneasily sideways a few times, looking at Mike. He was quite clearly in pain, and in spite of the fact that Mike barely touched him, the horse trembled and shuddered. I talked quietly to him, stroking his head and neck, partly to calm him down, and partly to distract him from Mike's attempts to find out exactly what was wrong.

Mike was squatting in the water, his hands feeling around along the bottom of the lake. He looked more and more worried.

"What is it? Did you find anything?"

"I think his leg is stuck between an old branch and some large stones. Goodness knows how we will get him free!"

Mike started to pull the branch, which made the horse even more anxious and tense. He snorted and moved his head violently, so violently that I nearly lost my balance and had to let go of the lead rope. The water reached up to my stomach.

I managed to get hold of the lead rope again, and I began stroking one of his ears – I knew that always calmed Fandango down whenever he was frightened. It worked and it did not take long before the horse lowered his head and started to relax.

I tried to chase away as many horseflies and mosquitoes as I could, but it was not easy. The afternoon sun was intensely hot, and what little air movement there had been earlier here by the lake, had disappeared. I kept an uneasy eye on the thunderclouds building up, covering more and more of the sky. As far back as I could remember I had been afraid of thunder, and the mere thought of standing here, in water up to my stomach, holding a frightened horse, and a very long way from the safety of my home, didn't exactly help.

Mike suddenly gave a shout – lost his balance and fell backwards with an enormous splash. The horse lifted his left hind leg with a jerk – he was free!

"WOW!" I exclaimed. "You did it! You did it! GREAT!"

Mike stood up. Soaked. But smiling. "I never thought we would do it! Now, let's go home."

We led the horse onto dry land. He was limping a bit, but apart from that he seemed all right.

"How the heck are we getting home?" I asked Mike as I opened my backpack, looking for my cell phone.

"We'll call your Dad and Hans, and they can pick us up with their truck. We can't walk all the way home with –"

"It's a good thing you have your cell," I said with relief. "I left mine at home."

Mike opened his backpack, looking for his.

"Ah – well, great!" he said. "I left mine in the car!"

"Oh, no! I don't believe it!" Before I could say any more, or Mike could answer, the first thunderclap rolled noisily and threatening all round us.

"Please – I want to get home!" I pleaded.

"Let's walk back to the car, with the horse," said Mike. "I think he can manage that."

It was beyond me how Mike could be so darn calm! I had pains in my stomach from fear; the fact that we had saved the horse suddenly seemed less important than the imminent thunderstorm!

"What's up with you?" asked Mike. "You're white as a sheet!"

"I'm scared of thunderstorms!" I mumbled.

Mike and the horse looked at me, and the horse pushed his warm nose gently against my arm as if to say: "It will be OK – don't worry." Mike took the lead rope from me.

"Come on – let's try and find some shelter. Thunderstorms don't hang around for long, and when it's over we can walk to the car and drive home."

I nodded without saying anything – I was very frightened. We walked away from the water, the horse limping behind us. Horses understand much more than we give them credit for, and I am quite certain he understood that we would help him. In spite of the fact that he must have been in pain, and in spite of the fact that he had obviously been mistreated by the people who stole him, he trusted us and followed us willingly, with the lead rope hanging loose. I am sure that he would have followed us, even if we had had no lead rope.

We came to a little hollow in the forest, surrounded by trees, but not as tall as the trees in the rest of the forest.

The ground was soft and warm – and dry. I sat down, leaning against a large stone. My legs felt like jelly, one moment I was too hot, the next I was too cold. My clothes were soaked, clinging to me. I shivered when I heard thunder rumbling far away.

Mike sat down next to me and put one arm round my shoulders, holding the lead rope in the other. The horse snorted a few times, put his nose to the ground, smelling it, and then, to my surprise, lay down on the soft ground.

I got a bit worried, but Mike said he thought the horse was tired. Nobody knew how long he had been in the water – or what had happened to him before then.

I looked skywards. All I could see was a huge, very dark and very ominous cloud, which seemed to be only a few feet above the treetops. It had become very dark, and the silence was complete. The pain in my stomach was more intense, and I snuggled up against Mike.

"It's OK," he said, hugging me. "We're safe here."

"How do you know that?" I whispered. At that very moment the most terrific lightning lit up the whole area for a fraction of a second, immediately followed by a tremendous thunderclap. It was as if someone had fired a huge cannon next to us, and it frightened me so much that I screamed. I put my hands in front of my face, wishing I were miles away!

"Safe!?" I said, and my voice was trembling with fear. "Safe? It is right overhead – and next time."

"We've done what we can," said Mike, quietly and calmly. "We are in a place, slightly lower than the rest, and where the trees are not as tall as the rest. It is…"

He didn't have time to finish before the next flash of lightning, intensely white and even sharper and worse than the last one, lit up the world. This time the thunderclap didn't wait; it came at the same time as the lightning. I bit my lip and stared at the horse in an attempt not to panic. The horse just lay there, in front of us, half-asleep as if this was the best and safest place in the whole world.

"There you are," said Mike, holding me tight, "He's not afraid. His instincts are telling him we're safe here. Don't be afraid." I nodded, and tried to smile. It *did* help a bit that the horse was so calm.

The next thunderclaps were not so strong, and even though I was still scared, I began to think we might survive the storm.

I don't know how long we sat there, waiting, but it felt like an eternity. I began to feel hungry – the water Mike had brought along had been drunk a long time ago. When the first big drops of rain started to fall, and the thunder began to fade away, we decided to start walking again. We were soaked through anyway, so we could hardly get more wet!

The horse got up with some difficulties, and a bit reluctantly. He was limping more than before. He walked slowly, head down, behind us. The only good thing was that the horseflies and mosquitoes had disappeared – I wasn't the only one not enjoying thunder and lightning!

The way back seemed to be even longer and more difficult. We couldn't follow the same way back – because of the horse we had to walk round some of the thick bushes we had literally ploughed our way through on the way to the lake. I really don't know how Mike managed to keep track of where we were in relation to the car; I know I didn't.

Just as we reached the clearing in the forest, the sun peeped out from behind a dark cloud, and the strip of blue sky got bigger and bigger. An enormous rainbow with clear, bright colors appeared – the biggest and brightest rainbow I have ever seen.

When we reached the old lumber road, things became easier, and before long we could see Mike's car. Never have I been so happy to see that old banger! I was so happy to see it that I just wanted to kiss it! The horse stopped, head still drooping, and Mike got into the car, looking for his cell.

For a few terrible seconds I thought he didn't have it, but he did, and he called Hans and Dad. I was holding the horse, who was now chewing some blades of grass. He was totally apathetic, as if he realized we had reached the end of our walk, and so what?

"You're a wonderful horse," I whispered to him, and stroked his neck. "How can anyone treat you like they have?"

The horse put his nose into my palm, and I remembered that Mike had some cubes of sugar, which I gave him. The horse ate them, and nosed me for some more. Which I thought was a good sign.

"We'll have to walk down to the gravel road," said Mike. "Hans can't drive his truck out here."

"But what about the horse?" I asked. "Where shall we put him? You don't have any stables."

"He'll have to be in a box at your house. Your mother is getting one ready now."

"But what about Fredrik's dad?" I said, and Mike looked at me.

"You're right!" he said. "I didn't think of that!"

My stomach pains returned. "What if he says it is his horse, and –" I said slowly.

"No!" said Mike with a firm voice. "No – there is no way he can claim the horse, unless he can *prove* it is his! We'll call the police the moment we get home."

I nodded, and we started walking. But in spite of Mike sounding so reassuring, I still felt nervous. Very nervous.

Chapter 12

"What the heck! Where on earth did you find that poor creature?"

Hans was the first one out of the cab, and looked at us in amazement. We arrived at the gravel road the moment Dad and Hans arrived in Hans's old truck.

"In the lake," I said, feeling exhausted.

"Don't be silly, Sara," said Dad uneasily. "Answer properly. Where *did* you find that horse? Whose is it? Where has he come from?"

"It's a long story," said Mike. "It all started –"

"Please!" I interrupted. "Let's get home first – *then* we can explain."

Dad and Hans nodded as one, and Hans opened the truck and let down the ramp. Dad took care of the horse by first removing the old, worn halter, replacing it with Maverick's soft leather halter. Then he led the horse to the truck; the horse walked up the ramp and into the truck without hesitation.

"He seems to have been in a truck before," said Hans and pushed the half-wall in position next to the bay. "Just

114

as well. It wouldn't have been much fun struggling with a strange horse here, in the middle of nowhere."

"Are you coming with us?" asked Dad, and I nodded.

"OK, I'll get my car and follow," said Mike, and as we turned the truck, I saw him running off towards his car.

On the way home I told Dad and Hans what had happened lately. The ride Sophia and I had, our first meeting with the horse, that we suspected Fredrik's dad was doing things he shouldn't do, and finally how Mike and I had spotted the horse in the lake some hours before.

Dad and Hans listened, and when I finished, Hans looked like the thundercloud we had just had overhead.

"That Frank!" he hissed. "If he's selling horses for slaughter, I'll have a word with him! Or two!" he added.

Dad nodded. "So will I!"

Mom, Maggie, and Sophia were waiting for us as we turned into our yard. And no sooner had we unloaded the horse than Mike came speeding in his car, braking hard and stopping in a cloud of dust.

Mom had made Maverick's large box ready for the horse, and he entered it, sighing deeply and audibly. He didn't show much interest in where he was or what was happening – he just stood there, head drooping. He touched neither the water nor the hay; he just looked tired and bedraggled.

Dad took our first aid box, and plenty of cotton wool, compresses, and puttees, and he and Hans cleaned the horse's wounds carefully. Mike and I once more told everyone what had happened that afternoon, and Sophia scowled at me when I finished.

"Why wouldn't you let me come along?" she asked me angrily. "It's typical! Just ignore me! As if I wouldn't have been able to help!"

"You weren't home!" I replied.

"So? Couldn't you have waited, or called me on the cell?"

"You wouldn't have enjoyed being in the middle of the forest in the thunderstorm, would you?" I asked.

Sophia snorted.

"At least I am not terrified of thunderstorms!" she said sarcastically, and was about to add something when Dad interrupted.

"The poor thing is running a temperature," he said to Hans, showing him the thermometer. "Over 100 degrees."

Hans nodded.

"I had a suspicion," he said, "being he seemed so listless. Have you called the vet?"

Maggie nodded. "Yes, but she was in the middle of something and couldn't be here for several hours."

Dad sighed.

"I'll call Karl Fransson," he said with a firm and determined voice. "Give me the cell!"

"But you can't disturb him in the middle of his holiday!" exclaimed Mom, but Dad had already made his mind up and rang the number of our regular, excellent and above all very kind vet.

"This is an emergency," Dad explained seriously, lifting the phone to his ear. We could hear the ringing tone.

"I don't think he will be annoyed," said Hans, looking serious. "I called him once in an emergency, and no problem."

"If only he were home!" I said, looking at the horse, which was standing quite still, head lowered, eyes half closed, resting his injured leg.

It seemed an eternity before Dr. Fransson answered. Dad explained quickly what it was, and the vet promised to come over right away.

As always when you wait for the vet to come to attend to a sick animal, it seems like hours. Mom suggested that Mike and I go in and change our clothes – Mike could borrow a pair of Dad's jeans and a sweater. Neither of us wanted to leave the horse, but when Dad said that we were really not much use, standing there, shivering, looking like drowned rats, we followed Mom into the house.

She made some sandwiches while we changed, and suddenly I realized I was very hungry. Mike and I took the sandwiches over to the stables just as the vet arrived in his old, red car. He parked next to Mike's, nodded to us, and walked across to the stables.

Camigo, Maverick, and Fandango were standing by the fence, following him with their eyes. I couldn't help laughing in the middle of it all when I saw how suspicious Fandango looked. He probably thought it was time for another flu vaccination. And if there is one thing my dear, old pony hates and is afraid of, it is injections!

Mike and I entered the stables behind the vet, who started the examination immediately. He felt and examined him carefully and thoroughly; the horse was standing still, listless. It didn't even bother him that the vet examined his injured leg, very carefully. A few twitches of the skin, and a deep sigh. Nothing else.

"What's his temperature?" Dr. Fransson asked Dad.

"103 degrees. Do you want me to take it again?"

"Yes, please. I'll get some things from the car in the meantime."

Dad went into the box, but before he could do anything, the horse laid heavily down on the straws, sighing audibly.

"Oh, no!" I whispered to Mike. "Do you think he'll die?"

117

"No, I don't," said Mike, putting one arm round my shoulder. But I could tell from his voice that he wasn't all that sure.

"Oh dear," said the vet, returning with a little bottle and a syringe. "He's laid down!"

"Shall we try and get him up?" asked Hans, but the vet shook his head.

"No, leave him. I can still give him this."

"What is it?" wondered Mom, who – as a nurse – spends half her days helping to vaccinate crying babies.

"It's tetanus vaccine," said the vet, injecting the horse with a skilled hand.

"Being we don't know where he comes from or whether he has been vaccinated at all, it is just as well to give him a dose," he added.

"But aren't you going to give him some more medication?" I asked uneasily.

The vet shook his head and stood up.

"No, there's not a lot I can do for the poor thing. We'll just have to wait and see."

"But what is *wrong* with him?" I asked. "Why is he lying down?"

The vet looked at the horse for a while, rubbed his chin thoughtfully and said: "I don't really know, but I think he's simply exhausted. He has been bitten to pieces by mosquitoes, and we don't really know how long he was in the water. And he does not seem to have been in top-form before all this happened, so…"

He paused and took his pipe out of his pocket. We left the stables, leaving the poor horse in peace for a while.

"Tell me again how you found him," said the vet, lighting his pipe. "I couldn't quite follow it all. Where did he come from?"

"It's a very long story," I said. The whole thing started when –"

"I think we should go in and have a cup of coffee," interrupted Mom, "and you can tell it all then."

Dr. Fransson nodded in agreement, and we walked over to the house.

The evening was drawing in. It was still warm, but not as close and humid as it had been before the thunderstorm. Mom quickly laid the garden table for coffee, and it wasn't until I sank down into the hammock next to Mike that I realized how exhausted I was. I ached all over, the mosquito bites on my arms and legs were stinging, and I struggled to keep my eyes open.

No sooner had we sat down than Dr. Fransson's cell rang. He muttered something that did not sound too pleasant, and answered it. The next second he shot up from his chair, and we all looked at him.

"OK – I'll be right over! Of course!" There was no need for him to tell us it was an emergency.

"I'm terribly sorry," he said, looking longingly at the cookies Mom had just put down on the table. "The horse of a friend of mine has managed to entangle himself in some barbed wire."

"Oh, dear," said Mom. "I hope he will be all right – but do drink your coffee at least before you take off."

"Thanks!" said Dr. Fransson and gulped the coffee down, still standing.

"What about the horse – the one in our stables?" I asked quickly. Dr. Fransson looked at me.

"Just take a look at him now and then, and take his temperature. If it goes up, or if he seems to get weaker, call me at once. If he manages to get up, that's a good sign," he added.

119

"Perhaps someone should be with him in the stables all of the time?" I asked. He nodded. "Yes, fine. As I said, call me immediately if he gets worse. But I must leave now."

"Gets worse?" I thought to myself, feeling a lump in my throat. The poor thing couldn't get much worse than he was.

Mike left for home with Hans and Maggie to collect his sleeping bag, and I went to my room and to lie down. I was aching all over after the struggle through the forest, and I knew I would be stiff and sore the following day. I must have dozed off for a while, because when someone knocked on my door, it startled me and it took a few seconds before I realized what it was.

It was Sophia. She had that ingratiating and super friendly look she often has when she wants something, and I got suspicious before she had uttered a single word.

"Mom says that you and Mike are spending the night in the stables," she said.

"That's right," I said quickly. "But you're not!"

"But my dear sister!" said Sophia with a velvety soft voice.

I looked at her. "Why would you want to spend the night in a rotten old stable? *YOU*, who are not interested in horses at all?"

"It's better there are more of us, isn't it?" she said. "What if the horse takes a turn for the worse, and…"

I cut her off. "In that case, I'll get Mom or Dad. It's as simple as that. I don't want you there, OK?"

"Mom said I could!" said Sophia defiantly. "So there! – And the stables aren't yours anyway. And Alexandra is coming as well!" she added curtly.

"Get lost!" I said angrily. "Are you crazy? The two of you sitting there chatting away all night, with that poor horse nearly on death's door? Never!"

"We can be quiet if we want to!" said Sophia haughtily and stalked out from my room. Without banging the door.

I tried to relax again, but I felt annoyed and couldn't. So I walked downstairs and found Mom on the veranda, reading a paper.

"Why did you say to Sophia that she could sleep in the stables?" I asked and sat down on the steps.

"Why not if she wants to?" said Mom, looking up from her paper. "There's plenty of space."

"Yes, but I don't want her there! And she is bringing Alexandra – the two of them will just sit there and babble and giggle all night. The horse needs peace and quiet!"

Mom nodded. "Yes, perhaps. But if they talk and giggle too much, just ask them to stop."

"They won't listen to me. You know what Sophia is like!"

"I think you're a bit unkind," said Mom quietly. "Does it matter if there are two or four sleeping there? I can't see the problem."

"Sleeping?" I hissed. "We're not going to sleep – we're going to keep a watchful eye on the horse in case he gets worse."

Mom sighed.

"OK, OK. But I have said yes to Sophia."

"I don't care!" I said and went indoors. Halfway up the stairs I met Sophia.

"Have a nice time in the stables tonight!" I said. "I'll stay in my bed instead."

"Good," said Sophia, grimacing at me with her tongue out.

I shut the door to my room behind me and looked out the window. Alexandra was just arriving on her bike, with a sleeping bag and a pillow tied to the little baggage-holder, and a small bag hanging from the handlebars. I could see the bright colors of bags of potato chips her bag.

Sophia greeted her, and the two of them stood chatting and gesturing. It seemed clear that Sophia told Alexandra that they would be all on their own in the stables, and that's when I made my mind up. Sophia and Alexandra obviously thought they were going to have some sort of private party in the stables all night; what if the horse deteriorated and they never noticed? Never! I decided then and there to spend the night in the stables.

We looked in on the horse now and then during the evening, apart from that we left him alone. He was standing, but he would not eat or drink anything. Dad had telephoned the vet and was told that if the horse hadn't had anything to drink by the next morning, we had to call the animal hospital.

Dad had also telephoned the police, and they had promised to come out to us the next morning to have a look. They were certain this was the horse that had been running around, nearly causing some accidents, but whose horse was it? The police didn't know either. They had not received any report about missing horses.

I had wanted Dad to tell the police about our suspicions concerning Fredrik's dad, but Dad didn't want to. He thought it was best to wait until the next day, when he could talk to them personally. A Saturday evening, he said, was hardly the most opportune time to ask the police to have a look at some badly treated horses, which made me quite angry.

I couldn't stop thinking about those poor horses in

Fredrik's dad's big building, without any food or water –
how many of them would be alive tomorrow? I hoped that
someone would have given them some water, at least – to
die from thirst is worse than to die from hunger, they say.
But I had a strong feeling I was hoping in vain.

Chapter 13

At about 11 p.m. we walked across to the stables and got ready for the night. I had cleaned out Maverick's box and put down a lot of clean straw, and we put our sleeping bags on top.

Sophia and Alexandra bedded down in a corner away from us, and Mike and I sat down where we could keep an eye on the horse to see whether he was laying down or standing up.

Sophia and Alexandra were in a giggling mood, although they tried to be serious. They were close together, eating chips, drinking soft drinks, giggling hysterically into their sleeping bags in the hopes that we wouldn't notice.

Mike and I played cards. We had lit the little stable lamp, which made it just about possible to see the cards and the horse, but not much more.

The horse had lain down again, and we went over and had a look at him. He seemed neither better nor worse; he was still lethargic and listless, and we agreed we should take his temperature every two hours or so.

I don't know what the time was, exactly, when Sophia suddenly sat bolt upright and gave a shout.

"Alexandra – I had clean forgotten…!"

"What? What is it?" asked Alexandra, equally loudly, obviously as startled as we were. "What's up?"

Sophia's shout and sudden movement had made the horse nervous – I could hear how he struggled to get on his feet.

"Idiots!" hissed Mike. "You said you would be quiet!"

"Ooops – sorry!" whispered Sophia. "But I forget there's a super film on TV at midnight. A real screamer!"

"Is it all right with your parents that we watch it then?" asked Alexandra, and Sophia nodded.

"Yes, I asked Mom earlier, and she said it was OK – she would probably watch it herself."

"Good," said Alexandra and yawned.

Both of them got out of their sleeping bags and gathered their chips and other goodies, quickly and quietly.

"Not so fast!" said Mike and grabbed a large, unopened packet of crisps from Sophia's hand as they walked past us. "We'll keep that one!"

"But –" said Sophia; then she laughed and shrugged her shoulders as they left the stables and walked across the yard in the warm and dark August evening.

"Your mother is quite cunning at times," said Mike and opened the packet as quietly as he could.

I agreed.

"I have a few goodies for us as well," said Mike, nodding towards his rucksack. "Hot chocolate and sandwiches."

We made ourselves a bit more comfortable, leaning against the box wall. Mike poured some hot chocolate into two mugs and unpacked the sandwiches – my favorites with cheese and tomato.

"Wonderful," I whispered, "I'm starving."

"It makes you hungry, I tell you. If only you knew how many nights I have been sitting in stables waiting for a mare to foal." He sighed. "We certainly didn't have such modern equipment as cable TV and things which Hans is having in his new stables."

I knew Mike's parents had a stud farm, and sitting there he told me a lot of exciting things from his childhood.

I became quite envious, because he had done a lot of all those things I was still dreaming of doing.

He had taken part in show jumping for many years – he had even competed abroad. He had broken in numerous young horses and ponies, and he had worked as an apprentice in some well-known stables and even ridden some thoroughbreds. Then he worked with horses abroad before he returned and started working for Hans and Maggie.

"But why did you end up here?" I asked.

Mike gave a little laugh.

"I have always preferred horses to schools, so I don't have a degree or any school diplomas. I did go to school, of course, but I left as soon as I possibly could and started working with horses instead."

"But how did you end up *here*, I meant, a little place in the middle of nowhere? Why here?"

"Hans told me that the people on the neighboring farm had a very pretty daughter!" he said jokingly and kissed my ear.

"Phooey!" I said and blushed. "Don't be silly! Tell me why!"

"OK. I wanted a job I could combine with studying," whispered Mike. "I want to take some exams and study a bit more."

"What do you want to do, then? Working with horses?"

I could see Mike nodding. "Yes. Well, I —" he hesitated a bit, "I'm really hoping to become a vet."

"But you need top marks to do that!" I said, louder than I intended.

"I know. But if I study hard enough —"

"But it is very, very difficult to become a vet," I said.

Mike nodded. "Yes, but if you want something, *really* want something badly enough, you can do it. And I want to help sick animals, or animals who are suffering. If you want to make your dreams come true, you have to work for it. You don't get anything free in this world."

He put his arm round my shoulders, and we sat there, quiet, a long time, leaning against the box wall. I thought of what he had just told me, his childhood, all the horses, competitions, and travels — and suddenly I was not envious any more, just determined to do the same things. Or *my* things, rather.

OK — I could not just pack my bags and go to another country to find work at the moment; but what about next summer? And compete. Unless I could find a proper and suitable horse, I would change to field competitions. Train a lot, and not be so lazy when it came to dressage, for example.

"What are you thinking?" asked Mike, his lips close to my ear.

"That I'll ride more dressage with Fandango," I said, and Mike laughed quietly.

"That can't do any harm," he said and got slowly up. "It's 2 a.m. — shall we take his temperature again?"

We entered the box, and Mike took the temperature. I stood by the horse's head, stroking his neck gently, but he didn't seem to care whatever we did to him. He stood absolutely still, head down, as if he were drugged.

127

"The temperature has gone up a bit," Mike whispered. It made me uneasy – I didn't have the remotest idea how high a temperature a horse could tolerate, but whatever it was, this was hardly a good sign.

We left the box, and hardly were we out before the horse lay down again, sighing loudly and painfully. He stretched his legs straight out and closed his eyes. I got really scared.

"Look at him!" I said to Mike, who looked as uneasy as I felt.

Mike went back into the box and squatted down, stroking his neck, probably to see if the horse would react. I was holding my breath.

The horse was lying very, very still, eyes closed, breathing heavily. My stomach knotted with fear. This did not look good at all.

Mike stroked the neck of the horse several times, without the horse reacting. Finally he hit the horse with the palm of his hand – the sound nearly made me jump. But the horse did not move – he opened his eyes for a second or two; then closed them again, breathing heavily.

"Oh, no!" I gasped.

I could feel tears running down my cheeks, and I swallowed several times to try and get rid of the lump in my throat. I wiped a few tears away with my hand.

"Do you think we ought to ring Dr. Fransson?" I asked.

Mike got up and looked at the horse. "Yes, I think we have to."

He came out from the box, found his cell and punched the number.

"I'll get Mom and Dad," I said, and Mike nodded.

I was crying when I ran across the yard and into the house. It was quiet and dark nearly everywhere, only the sitting room had a light on – and the TV was on. And in the corner of the settee were Sophia and Alexandra sound asleep like two little piglets. I closed the door carefully not to wake them.

I took a deep breath, dried my tears, and walked upstairs to my parent's room.

Both of them woke up as soon as I opened the door, and it did not take many minutes before all three of us were in the stables. Mike got a hold of Dr. Fransson, who said he would come immediately.

I looked into the box. The horse was lying just like he was when I left him, now breathing with difficulties. Dad shook his head.

"This doesn't look good at all," he said. Mike agreed.

"I tried to make him stand up," said Mike, "but he either can't or he won't."

"Let's just wait until the vet comes," said Mom. "Perhaps it isn't *quite* as bad as it looks." She tried to cheer us all up.

I could feel the tears coming back, and couldn't stay there any longer so walked out into the fresh air. Dawn had just started breaking, it was pleasantly warm and the grass was topped with dew. Camigo and Maverick had lain down, but Fandango was standing, half-asleep. He spotted me, neighing lazily and came towards me.

I put my arms round his neck, buried my face in his mane and sobbed, tears streaming. I thought of all those poor hungry and thirsty horses in that big machinery building, the dying horse in our stables, and all other suffering horses.

I cried and cried and the tears were flowing as if they were never going to stop. Fandango stood quite still and let me hold him. He seemed to understand my grief – normally he would be playful and start teasing me.

The lights from a car turning into our drive made me let go of Fandango. I dried my tears with the sleeve of my sweater, and took a deep breath. Fandango pushed me gently with his muzzle, and I couldn't help but laugh at him. It was as if he asked: "Are you all right now?" No wonder I loved Fandango – he really was wonderful.

I gave him a quick hug before I went back to the stables, arriving at the same time as Dr. Fransson.

The lights were on in the stables, and Dr. Fransson walked straight over to the box without stopping. Looking worried, he squatted by the horse, stroking his head and neck, just like Mike had done earlier. Then he listened to his heart and lungs, and examined the horse as best he could.

"Does he have a temperature?" Dad wondered.

"Yes, I think so," said Dr. Fransson. He sounded unhappy.

I had to swallow to prevent myself from screaming in fear. There was total silence in the stables, all of us standing there, looking at the poor horse lying apparently lifeless on the straws. I wondered if he *was* dead already – I bit my lips so I would not start crying again.

Suddenly, very suddenly, the horse opened his eyes and looked surprised. It was just as if he had woken up, not knowing where on earth he was! He lifted his head, rolled over onto his stomach and made some snorting noises. I gripped Mike's hand – hard.

"That's it – good boy, good boy!" said Dr. Fransson, and the horse snorted again. "We'll get you OK again."

"People can recover even after severe stress and illness, given time," said Mom quietly. "So perhaps horses can as well."

"That's right," said Dr. Fransson. Just then the horse tried to get up.

At first he had difficulties finding his balance; he remained sitting, half up, half down, swaying back and forth.

"Take it easy! Take it easy!" said Dad, encouraging him. "There's no hurry, old boy!"

The horse snorted several times, threw his head from side to side in an irritated manner – then using all his force, heaving and pushing – and suddenly he was standing on all four legs again!

"Well, I'll be darned!" mumbled Dr. Fransson, suddenly sounding hopeful. "He got up by himself. That's a good sign!"

I couldn't hold back the flood of tears any more. But this time they were tears of joy – not sorrow.

The horse took a faltering step, put his nose into the water container – and drank, and drank, and drank. Then he sniffed the hay – and took a mouthful! That crunching sound when he chewed the hay was the nicest, best, happiest sound I had ever heard!

"What's the matter, Sara?" asked Mom. "You're crying."

"I'm so – so happy!" I snuffled. "He'll be all right now, won't he?"

The vet laughed, patting the horse's neck. He sounded relieved. "Yes, he'll be OK. The danger is over."

"I thought he would die," said Mike slowly. "I have never seen a horse that ill before."

"He was very, very ill, but you never know," said the vet. "If the heart decides to give up, the show is over." He made it clear that it had been a very close call.

We stood in silence, a long time, looking at the horse that walked slowly around in his box, investigating, wondering. He took a few more mouthfuls of hay – and lay down again on the soft straw. But he didn't sigh and breathe heavily like he had done before; he looked tired more than anything else. He yawned, opening his mouth so wide that we couldn't help laughing.

Dr. Fransson was also tired. He yawned nearly as wide as the horse, putting his stethoscope into one of his pockets.

"And now, my friends, I am off to go home. Let me know if you have any problems."

"I promise," I said. "Do you think we should continue to watch him?"

"By all means," yawned the vet again, "if you can, it would be a good idea if someone could stay here until morning."

So we did. Mike and I crept into our sleeping bags, while Mom and Dad went back to bed. Daylight had reached the stables, and the August morning was beautiful. I stretched, yawned and dozed off – and that's the moment I heard it.

It was a very strange and eerie sound I had never heard before – and it came from the horse's box.

"Mike!" I whispered, and I think he noticed I was frightened. "Can you hear it? Listen – it's a strange noise. Do you think we ought to ring Dr. Fransson again?"

Mike listened a while – and laughed.

"I think Dr. Fransson is a darn good vet – but I bet he will agree that even he can't cure a horse of snoring!"

Chapter 14

"Why didn't you wake us?"

Sophia's sharp voice woke me with a jolt, and I opened my eyes. It took a few seconds before I realized where I was or what had woken me so suddenly. I was not really in the habit of waking up in Fandango's box, lying in a sleeping bag!

Mike was already up – his sleeping bag hanging neatly over the wall of the box. I yawned and tried to get out of my bag; the zip had snagged so it took some wriggling before I succeeded.

"Why didn't you wake us?" demanded Sophia again. "Typical! Whenever something happens, you leave me out!" She sounded like a sulky 5 year old.

"There was no need to wake you," I said. "Stop moaning, will you? You could have stayed out here with us awake all night, watching the horse, instead of going in watching some stupid film or the other!"

"Hi! So you're awake," Mike's cheerful voice stopped Sophia from saying something. Mike peeped over the wall just as I was standing up, brushing bits of straw off my jogging suit.

I looked up – and saw the most wonderful sight! The horse was standing in Maverick's box, looking at me with great curiosity, ears pricked up, and eyes very bright and alert. It was probably the first time he had seen a heap of blue material turn into a human being.

"Oh, look! It's unbelievable!" I said and hurried over to the box. Mike laughed.

"He's improving by the hour. He has eaten – *and* had some water."

I looked at the horse, feeling happy. Very happy. But Sophia had no intention of letting the subject rest.

"Sshhhs!" she hissed. "I'll remember this! You just wait until you want me to help you."

"That will be a long wait," I replied. "Tell me, when was the last time you helped me with something?"

Sophia snorted angrily and stalked out from the stables. I really couldn't care.

"Come on – let's get some breakfast," said Mike. "I'm starving!"

My stomach told me it was time I fed it, so I nodded.

"The police will be here about 2 p.m. to look at the horse," said Mike as we hurried over to the house. "Then we can tell them about the horses in the machinery building as well. They will *have* to do something about it when they see them."

"Good!" I said, feeling there might still be some hope for those poor horses.

When we came into the kitchen, I saw to my surprise that it was past 10 a.m. Mom had the breakfast ready; the smell of newly brewed coffee and hot toast made my mouth water. And she had put my favorite marmalade on the table as well – the one that tasted more of lemon than of oranges.

Mike and I enjoyed every mouthful – and we took quite a few. When I finished, I felt like I would not be able to get up from my chair.

"I really enjoyed that," I said. "It was delicious!"

Mike gave my statement his full and enthusiastic support.

We helped clear the table, after which we walked to the stables again to see how the horse was doing.

Mike left for home a little later, and I took a quick shower before I made myself comfortable in the hammock. I started to read the book I never seemed able to finish, but the soft breeze, and the slight movement of the hammock, soon sent me into a deep and restful sleep.

I was rudely awakened by someone shaking the hammock violently.

"Wake up, you lazy thing!" shouted Sophia.

"What is it? What's up?" I struggled to open my eyes.

Sophia tipped the hammock right round, and I fell out, hitting the ground with a thud!

"What *are* you doing, you fathead! You could have killed me!"

Sophia laughed.

"Hardly! You had better wake up; the police will be here any minute."

I got up – slowly in case I had broken something – and walked into the house. Mom was sitting on the veranda, drinking a cup of coffee, and I was excited to see there was more in the kitchen. I poured myself a cup and joined Mom. She looked at me and frowned.

"You shouldn't really drink coffee, Sara. It's not good for you at your age."

"I don't drink that much. And I use lots of milk and sugar."

Mom sighed. "You ought to leave the sugar out as well."

"Mom," I replied. "I have seen many pictures of you as a young girl – with a cup of coffee in one hand, a cigarette in the other, hair dyed jet black, heavy make-up and-."

"Well…I was young and very stupid then. Now, I am older and wiser, and I am hoping that you and Sophia will be able to learn from my mistakes instead of having to find out for yourself." Mom always had an answer to everything.

About 2 p.m. Mike arrived in his car. He had only just parked his car when a police cruiser arrived, parking next to his old car. A young male police officer with a blonde mustache got out – my guess was that he had grown the mustache in order to look a bit older. Somehow he gave me a feeling that I could trust him.

We walked across to the stables. And when I say "we," it really was Mom, Dad, Sophia, Mike, and I – plus the police officer whose name was Andrew Roos.

He seemed to be used to horses, and studied the horse that was standing in the box, half-asleep. The moment he realized we were there he opened his eyes and came across to greet us. The police officer stroked his head and neck gently.

"Well, well, where do you come from?" he asked in a friendly way, as if the horse could answer him.

"Do you know who owns him or how he ended up here?" This time he addressed the questions to us.

"No," said Mom, "as I mentioned over the telephone – we have no idea."

"But I think I know where he comes from, at least," I said.

"And so do I!" added Sophia quickly, and I was rather pleased that she managed to be in on part of the story.

"Good," said Officer Roos, shutting the door. "Tell me, right from the beginning. I'll just have to get my notebook from the car."

We all went back into the warm, nice sunshine outside. That's when I saw a cloud of dust getting closer. It was Fredrik and his parents returning from the competition. Suddenly the sun didn't seem warm at all – my mouth went dry and I felt chilly all over.

What would happen if Fredrik's dad saw the horse in our stables? And what would his reaction be if he got to know that Mike and I had seen the terrible conditions of the horses in his big building? And what if he took the horse back to the others – and, I started feeling faint, cold, and very unhappy.

When Fredrik's mom turned into the yard with the car and trailer, we were all standing by the police car. Officer Roos had just succeeded in finding a pen that worked. Fredrik's dad saw us through the car window, and the car had hardly stopped when he jumped out.

"Hello!" he said, doing his best to sound friendly and interested. "What's up? I hope it's nothing serious."

"Sara and Mike have found a horse," said Mom and smiled. "A bay horse."

"Well, I'm ready!" said Officer Roos. "Now tell me the story!" He looked at Sophia and me.

Sophia did not have to be asked twice.

"One day Sara and I were out riding, we came across a newly built road, which Sara wanted to follow—," she started. She went on to describe how we followed the road, how we arrived at the large building, talked to Fredrik's dad, and then left.

Officer Roos looked expectantly at Fredrik's dad, writing down every word Sophia said. He thought no doubt that it was an extraordinary coincidence that the very person we were talking about should have arrived just then.

"Yes, and I asked the girls to keep away," said Fredrik's dad in a gruff voice, looking at me with angry eyes. "We were erecting a machinery building, and I didn't want them to be involved in an accident with the trucks."

"So when did you see the horse, then?" asked Officer Roos, looking at me.

Now it was my turn to explain how we had been forced off the road and into the ditch by the two trucks, how we heard a horse shrieking – and how the horse had come tearing along the road only minutes later.

"So the horse came from you, did it?" asked the police officer, pointing to Fredrik's dad with his pen. "Is it your horse?"

Fredrik's dad went purple in the face.

"Eh – I don't exactly recognize –"

"But why did you bring a horse along to a machinery building in the middle of a forest?" asked Mom, looking genuinely surprised. "Why didn't you take him to the stables?"

"Well, yes – but –"

Fredrik's dad fell silent, looking more and more irritated, his face getting even redder. He was visibly perspiring, and I could see the blood vessels on the side of his forehead swelling.

Finally he cleared his throat. "Well, let me say it as it is. That big building is to be used to house animals for slaughter during the summer. I didn't want to tell the girls that, you know how little girls are with animals."

"Horses as well?" I asked, pretending I didn't know already. "Do you have horses there?"

"Yes, but only temporary. The building is really intended

138

for cattle. But I got the chance to buy some horses for slaughter from Finland and Estonia, and since it sounded like a good business-deal –" He shrugged his shoulders, and added, "Horsemeat is quite popular now, of course, what with the mad cow disease and all that."

"Do you have permission to have horses in the building?" asked Officer Roos, and Fredrik's dad nodded.

"Yes. I had a vet inspect the building only last week, so all is in order." he said, "and now I suggest we unload the pony and take the horse back with us."

"But it's not your horse!" I exclaimed. "It has been stolen."

"Listen, little girl!" hissed Fredrik's dad. "Don't tell lies! If it is a bay with a white mane, it is mine. I have the receipt!"

"But I have a picture of the horse in a newspaper," I said quickly to the police officer. "It is a Finnish trotter, stolen in Finland some weeks ago."

"Hmh," said the officer. "Are you sure?"

"It is not true!" said Fredrik's dad angrily. "Don't listen to her! The girl is well known for making up wild stories! She is in my son's class at school, and she is very envious of his competitive abilities and –"

"I'll get the newspaper!" I said. "Wait! Don't let him take the horse, *please!*"

"Don't worry," said the police officer, "We'll wait here – *all* of us," he added, looking at Fredrik's dad.

I rushed into the house, flung the door open, and ran up to my room, two steps at a time. Last time I saw the newspaper it was on my desk. All I had to do was collect it, show it to the police officer, and…

The paper wasn't there.

"Oh, NO!" I shouted, staring at the empty desk. I could

not believe my eyes! Who had taken the paper? Where was it? Where *was* the paper?! It had been here, in my room, and nobody would normally go in and take anything.

Then I suddenly remembered Mom had said something about taking the papers down to the recycling area. Oh, no! She must have seen the paper, looked at the date, and –

I ran downstairs so fast that I nearly fell flat on my face, and out onto the verandah where we kept the boxes we put old papers in. They were not there!

I burst out crying, feeling confused, miserable, and desperate. What should I tell them, how could I?

I met Dad in the door.

"What's the matter, Sara?" he asked. "You look terrible."

"The newspaper!" I cried. "The paper – it's gone! Mom has taken it to the recycling area, the one –"

Dad laughed.

"Take it easy, young lady. The boxes with the papers in are in the back of the car. Mom hasn't had time yet."

Both of us ran to the car – and there – I could hardly believe it – there were three cardboard boxes full of newspapers. I started frantically to look through one of them, and Dad looked through another. But it wasn't until we were half way down box number three that we found what we were looking for.

My hands were trembling when I opened it, and Dad studied the picture of the horse intensely. Then he nodded.

"No doubt about it – that's the same horse," he said, patting my shoulders. We ran back to the others.

They had gone into the stables again, and were standing in front of the box where the horse was. Fredrik's dad was arguing fiercely with the police officer because he wouldn't let him take the horse, but he clammed up when he saw Dad and me coming with the paper.

The officer looked at the paper and studied the picture very closely. Then he read the article.

"Would you bring the horse out so I can take a closer look at him?" he asked Dad, who quickly put the halter on the horse and led him out in the open.

"Hmm," said the officer. "It would appear to be the same horse."

"It's a lie!" shouted Fredrik's dad angrily. "I bought the horse at an auction for horses for slaughter, and –"

"Well, yes, that may be so," said the police officer calmly, "but it may well have been stolen nevertheless. It is not unusual."

"You may put the horse back in now," he said to Dad. The horse followed Dad willingly.

"Do you have any more horses in that building?" the police officer asked Fredrik's dad, who didn't answer.

"Do you?" The officer looked at him.

"Not that it is any business of yours, but – yes, I do," he hissed. "What is the name of your boss, please? I intend to go right to the top with this, you wait and see! You won't be a police officer for much longer, I can promise you."

"Well, well, we'll see," replied the officer quietly.

"Why don't we all go over there and have a look? Now?" said Sophia suddenly. We all looked at her.

I swallowed.

"It's none of your bloody business!" exploded Fredrik's dad, staring as Sophia. "I have all the documents in order. The building is approved for housing animals. If you go there, you are trespassing on private property."

"I don't know why you are making such a fuss about it if you have nothing to hide!" said Sophia, staring back at Fredrik's dad. I had to look at her – I was quite impressed!

"I think my daughter is right," said Dad and put one arm

around her shoulders as if to protect her. "If all is in order –
what's the problem?"

"If you won't let us in voluntarily," said the police officer,
"I'll arrange for a search warrant on the basis of what I have
been told." He shut his notebook. "I have reasons to believe
that you have several horses in there who may be hungry,
which will make it easy for me to get such a warrant."

"Fine!" Fredrik's dad swore and turned to his wife and
Fredrik.

"Let's go right away."

We left as soon as they had unloaded Buzy Bee. Fredrik's
dad led the way, and – I promise you – he drove like a joy
rider! Then followed the police car, with Mike, Dad, Sophia
and me, and close behind came Mom in her car.

When we stopped outside the big building, I felt a mixture of relief and unease. What had happened to the horses?
Were they still alive?

Fredrik's dad stood by the door at the front of the building and waited. When I met his eyes, full of fury and hate,
I could feel my stomach churn over in sheer fright – in
spite of the fact that I knew he could do nothing but shout
and rant and look utterly unpleasant.

"OK!" he said angrily and opened the door. "Please go
in and have a look."

One thing was certain, I thought afterwards – if
Fredrik's dad had fully realized what we would see, he
would probably never have let us in.

The stench was unbelievable – far worse than when
Mike and I had had a quick look the day before. It was
stinging my nose, and my eyes filled with tears like they do
when you smell ammonia.

There were horses everywhere – in every box. Large
horses, small horses. All mixed together. Many of them

were lying down, some on their side, legs out, as if they were dead. Others were standing up, head drooping, listless. One horse had pushed his head through the railing – and got stuck, pulling desperately to get loose. A couple of horses neighed quietly when they saw us – a few more tried to join in, but otherwise; total, eerie silence.

Fredrik's dad swore again and walked quickly to a small office in one corner of the building. Through a window we could see two of the four men Mike and I had seen, sitting smoking and laughing.

They followed Fredrik's dad reluctantly out from the office, while he was ranting and raving at them. They waved their arms and shrugged their shoulders as if they were saying, "What is the matter? It's not our fault!"

Officer Roos stood by his police car, dialing his cell. I guessed he was asking for a vet and some reinforcements. I had never seen Dad so angry before in my life. He started in on Fredrik's dad.

"The horses need water! Can't you see they are dying?"

Frank Carlson glared angrily at Dad.

"Water's on the way!" he shouted, spreading both arms wide. "These idiots haven't bothered to fill the water tank. I shouldn't have to tell them to do so!"

"What?" said the youngest one. "What are you talking about? Which water tank? We're driving the horses to Denmark tonight, you said."

"Shut up, you fool!" screamed Fredrik's dad at him, looking as if he were going to have a heart attack.

"So there's no water here?" asked the police officer. Before anyone could reply, the unpleasant, female vet came in the door – followed by Dr. Fransson!

She carried a thick folder of documents. I wondered why, but I soon found out.

"This is the vet who inspected the building," said Frank Carlson, pointing to her. "She said it is OK. I telephoned her on the way over here – she'll show you that it is all in order!"

"Will I? It is hardly in order when the horses do not have any water, is it?" she asked sarcastically. "Turn on the water immediately – this is cruelty to animals!"

The older of the two men walked over to a tap on the side of one of the boxes and turned it. It creaked and squeaked – but nothing happened.

"You said you had installed water here?" said the vet angrily to Frank Carlson.

"Eh – no – I said a water tank!" hissed Frank Carlson back. "I said I would use a water tank until the water pipes had been laid."

"It says in these documents that you *have* installed water," the vet said, pointing to the bundle. "When I was here, inspecting it all, we agreed that no animal would be allowed into the building until it had running water."

Frank Carlson didn't answer. He just stood there, opened and closed his mouth, as if he were chewing something.

Dr. Fransson looked at his colleague, who started to look pale.

"Didn't you test the taps when you were here?"

She shook her head.

"No…I saw the drawings and they seemed in perfect order. I couldn't imagine that he would lie to me," she said, defending herself.

"OK," said Dr. Fransson and sighed. "There is no time to lose – the horses need water and air! Open all the doors, *wide*! And we need water – quickly! So, let's take care of the poor things!"

"I rang the firehouse," said Officer Roos. "They're

144

bringing a tanker full of water – they should be here any minute now."

Dr. Fransson went from horse to horse, looking at each one. He shook his head. "It's already too late for many of them. You'd better call the animal hospital as well, and ask them to send someone with the right equipment, I'm afraid."

"I've already done that," said Officer Roos quietly.

Chapter 16

When the tanker arrived, with flashing blue light and a tank full of water, we had already left. Dad stayed behind, and Hans had arrived, but Mom, Mike, Sophia, and I drove home.

We sat silent in the car; none of us said a single word. Sophia cried a little, but tried not to show it, and Mike held my hand and squeezed it tightly.

I wanted to cry, but couldn't. There was a big lump in my throat of sorrow and sadness, and no matter how many times I swallowed the lump wouldn't go away.

Mike gave me a long and good hug when we arrived home and before he drove back to his cottage on Hans and Maggie's farm. I walked slowly into the house and found Sophia on the settee in the sitting room, crying and sobbing her eyes out, with Mom beside her, one arm around her shoulders.

I went up to my own room without saying anything, and lay down. I ached all over from exhaustion, but I could not go to sleep. My head was buzzing – what we had seen this afternoon was so repulsive, so – so... My brain couldn't describe it – it was simply beyond words and description that anyone could even *think* of treating animals like that.

Suddenly I realized what I had to do. I hurried downstairs and into the stables. Fandango was standing near the gate. It really was as if he anticipated what I was going to do! Once more I began to seriously wonder if he could read my thoughts – even from a distance!

I saddled and quickly got him ready, and within minutes I was riding towards the forest. Fandango seemed eager. He started to trot, and I let him trot, which soon changed to a canter. I steered him into the forest, following the paths we both knew so well. We were like one, Fandango and I, and when we arrived on the forest road where Sophia and I always used to race each other, I loosened the reins and let Fandango go as fast as he wanted.

He ran flat out, the wind blowing his mane in my face, making my eyes water. Wonderful! Fandango didn't stop before we reached the end of the road.

"You're a darling!" I whispered in his ears and patted his sweaty neck. "You're the best in the whole world."

Fandango snorted, pleased with my praise. My eyes suddenly filled with tears again, and I let them stream freely down my cheeks, dripping onto Fandango. And Fandango, who always, always, jumps and kicks a bit after such a fast and long canter, carried me quietly home at a slow pace. He sensed we were not in a hurry. The sun sent warm rays down between the trees, all round us was the soft, beautiful smell of forest, a gentle wind cooled my face and dried my tears, and suddenly I halted Fandango.

In a spruce, close to the road, a blackbird was sitting motionless. He looked at us with his peppercorn eyes for quite a while – then he started singing. A lovely, thrilling blackbird song.

Fandango, who normally can't stay still for a second, didn't move a muscle, and gradually my feeling of sadness and sorrow gave way to a feeling of frustration and anger – anger at how we humans treat the animals. And there and then, sitting on Fandango in the middle of the forest, I swore and promised that I would do everything in my power to stop the awful animal transports over long distances to slaughterhouses all over Europe.

I had no clear idea how, but I knew that all horse lovers among us must stop this terrible trade. And not only horses but also calves, cattle, pigs and other animals. They all have feelings, and they all suffer!

The blackbird flapped his wings and flew off, and Fandango made a startled move. Then he lowered his head and tried to eat some grass, and he shook his head in a very irritated way when I stopped him. We set off again towards home. I stroked his neck and let him set the pace, and before long we left the forest behind.

Maverick and Camigo were asleep in their paddock. The afternoon sun threw long shadows across the fields, full of nearly ripe harvest, announcing that autumn was not all that far away. And with autumn, school started again.

A few days later we had an unexpected visit from a weather-beaten, slim man, dressed in jeans and a shirt, with short, grayish hair and blue eyes.

When the horse spotted him coming into the stables, he neighed loudly and got very excited; we could see immediately that the two – man and horse – had missed each other.

The visitor had tears in his eyes, stroking the horse over his head and along his neck, again and again, and the horse snorted and neighed gently – as if he were telling the man all that had happened!

148

His name was Erik Salmela. He was the manager of a large stud farm from where the horse and many other horses had been stolen.

Mr. Salmela had arrived in a large horse transporter – with the name of the stud farm in large letters on the sides – to collect "our" horse and the other horses belonging to the farm. All of them had survived – it was a miracle – in spite of the terrible things they had been through, and Mr. Salmela was very grateful.

Of course he wanted to know exactly what had happened and, when we had finished, he told us about the horse we had in a box in our stables. Täthivalo had won all the big races there were to win; he was priceless as a stud and had already sired many winners. Neither Mr. Salmela, nor any of us, could even begin to understand how anyone could steal him, or any of his stable mates, in order to sell them to a cheap price for slaughter.

After the horses were stolen, they were transported to an unknown market and sold at auction, far from home. A horse dealer had bought them and quickly sold them to Fredrik's dad – together with a lot of other horses from Finland and Estonia. All told he had bought about 35 horses – all of which were to be transported by trucks to somewhere much further south in Europe – for meat. The police succeeded in rolling up a long chain of horse thieves, dealers, and transporters, who had all cooperated in order to make money.

We were talking for several hours before Erik loaded the horse into his trailer.

The horse walked happily behind his master up the ramp, making himself comfortable by one wall, while Mr. Salmela put up the intermediate wall. He told us that Täthivalo had always stood in the same place during his competition-days, and the horse looked at him and seemed to say, "Come on, hurry up, or we'll be late!"

The last thing Mr. Salmela did before he jumped into the cab was to hand me a large, wrapped parcel. When we opened it, we stared straight at Täthivalo's face – a large, beautifully framed color photo of him at the height of his career.

When I saw the picture, my eyes filled with tears again. You could hardly believe this was the same horse as the one Mike and I rescued from the lake a week earlier, scraggy and half-dead. The white mane was flowing in the wind, his eyes were shining and you could actually *see* how proud and pleased he was, being the fastest – the winner!

"What does the name Täthivalo mean?" Mom asked, and Mr. Salmela laughed.

"Starlight," he said. "It's the Finnish word for the light which comes from the stars."

When Mr. Salmela finally drove off, we had a feeling that we waved good-bye to two very good and close friends.

And what about the other horses? Some, unfortunately, did not survive, and had to be put down where they were.

The police managed to trace all the owners of the surviving horses, and they were all transported back to Finland in a large, splendid horse-coach, and their respective owners collected them from some stables just outside Helsinki.

And after that there were 10 horses left, bought in a proper way by Fredrik's dad, and which he might send to slaughter if he wanted to. But he didn't get a chance.

The whole, awful story made the front page in our local paper, as well as in the national papers, so Fredrik's dad simply sold the horses to anyone who wanted to buy them.

The riding school bought one pony and a Fjord horse,

150

and as far as I know they are used for lessons. A kind, old lady who competes in dressage now and then, bought one of the workhorses from Estonia, while three Shetland ponies were bought by a family loving ponies. The four horses left were taken in by Hans and Maggie until they got good homes in the neighborhood.

And what about Fredrik's dad? He was arrested for theft, receiving stolen property, and the mistreatment of animals – all of which totally destroyed his reputation as someone who cared for and looked animals! True, he has another big farm, but the latest I heard was that he sold all his animals and started to grow oats instead.

And they did not move into their new, elegant place either, but sold it. Fredrik's mom got so angry when she realized what her husband had been involved in, that she divorced him. Although, I have a sneaking suspicion that the main reason was that Fredrik's dad lost an awful lot of money and his good name, and not so much that she was all that sorry for the horses.

Anyway, she and Fredrik now live in an apartment in town, and Buzy Bee is still kept at the riding school – where the girls still think Fredrik is God's gift to women, and are more than willing to take care of his pony.

And, finally – what about our new stables? Well, nothing! None of us cared to lift a hand any more during the last week when Dad started work again. And in only a few days, school starts again, so…

The container with all the rubbish was taken away and emptied, but Mom and Dad carried all the other bits and pieces back into the cowshed again, so the yard wouldn't look so messy. And not only that, a few other things were also carried over to the cowshed, such as Mom's old clay pots, Sophia's chair, which she no longer wanted in her room, some cardboard boxes full of books, which Mom originally had intended to give to the Red Cross – and a lot more.

But, as Dad said when he closed the cowshed door behind him the other day,

"At least it has been thoroughly cleaned – that's a good start if we're going to make this place into stables one day!"

P.S. Oh, I forgot to mention that Sophia never dated Fredrik! She has fallen for a guy who loves sports, and just now she peeped into my room, dressed in a new jogging suit – and with make-up on! She and Alexandra have taken up jogging, and she wanted to borrow my blue jogging shoes, to save her ruining her new, white Nike sneakers.

She is hopeless!